D1526155

I the Son

An Anthology of Poems, Short Stories, Songs and Slices of Life

By Darryl V. Smith

Dvsimagines Publishing

Acknowledgments

I would like to offer a special thanks to some people who inspired, encouraged, and participated in the creation of this work: Sidney Johnson, a realer brother and better friend I could not find; My mother, Gloria Ivery for always making me believe that God was bigger than my problems, and for always keeping me before the Lord in prayer; and an extra special thanks to my children Teharah, Mallorie (and her little Madison Jolee) and Benjamin Smith; my arrows, a fuller quiver could not be obtained. Finally, to Jackie: the love of my life. Thank you for reading, listening, and more importantly occasionally 'pushing'. You are an awesome woman that I am blessed to have as my wife.

Cover concept and design by D. Smith and the late great Jeniel Smith

Final cover production by Damon Reed

One Night…

On the phone with my God-sister

Time: 11:37pm

Her: "What else you been up to, we haven't talked in a while…"

Me: "Just messing around, writing poems and stories and stuff…"

Her: "Really...you write? Let me hear one."

(3 poems and a short story later)

Her: "Oh my God, that was really good. I could picture what was happening in my mind! You need to write a book or something!"

Sometimes the birth of a thing is nourished by the encouragement of a friend.

Thank you April Anderson Dudley for listening.

Preface

Over the years I have come to grips with who I am. Although I have many interests and hobbies, at the heart of it all I am an artist. I started as a kid drawing in Chicago's worse housing project, the Robert Taylor Homes until I graduated from 8th grade. In truth I could do most anything with my hands; whether it was building complex model cars and airplanes or painting and designing and constructing things (I later made props and designed sets for plays). In high school and college I excelled in music (sax and woodwinds) and enjoyed playing jazz, classical and gospel music with great passion.

I never considered myself a writer though. As a musician I wrote music and lyrics for songs I heard in my head but as I got older, writing lyrics evolved into poetry and finally short stories. It became the secret way I wrote down my ideas, feelings and perceptions. It was the way I processed thoughts and pain and in truth, it probably kept me from going crazy. Also, I wrote to not only artistically express myself but to also convey thoughts I did not feel comfortable saying out loud. As a male growing up in 70's I was taught to suppress my emotions, stuff them down and become hard. As life broke my emotional concrete, I slowly opened and wrote. It became the secret unknown language of my soul.

I loved writing poetry because it's like me, it's not perfect. Poetry doesn't have to be exact and I could have liberties with style, words and invention. I used it especially to put my feelings out there without it being obvious that I was in pain or trying to work through the madness of life. I played with different styles, and soon worked on short stories and slices of life, like the Rev. Theolopheous' sermon. Each section is focused on a different part of the human experience; my human experience.

The 'My Life Mine' chapter is about my family and my evolution and growth to the title piece 'I the Son'. 'I Saw the Lord' is my spiritual journey and speaks of purpose and destiny that only God can give. 'In The Beginning' is my disrespect for death while accepting his realities. 'My Neighborhood' is my social world around me. It is my urban swimming pool in which I have swum my entire life: Black folks, poor folks powerless and betrayed. 'Show em' is an anthem to stop feeling sorry or sad for yourself, shake it off and fight for the right to be what you are born to be. It's my fist in the air, understanding that the struggle to succeed is internal. 'Love lost love', my biggest section is my heart. It is full of past secrets, present circumstances, and future desires. Finally, since I am a self-diagnosed attention deficient disorder (ADD) person, I few random pieces, thoughts and odds and ends that never made it into anything but, well, the ADD section.

I don't know if what's in the following pages is considered 'good', great or otherwise. I didn't write it for the purpose of money (although I'm hopeful), fame or even literary acclaim. I wrote it because it is in me. Like you, I have an internal need to use the gifts I have been given. I have a love for words, how they fit and the wonderful diversity in people and their personalities and struggles.

I the Son is from my soul. It is what was/is in me. Pieces of me that have been squashed for years by a society that raised a cold detached black man, reconnected emotionally by God through time. I consider myself like most people. I hope you hear yourself in it, or you can at least I hope enjoy the effort.

Darryl

TABLE OF CONTENTS

MY LIFE MINE

I SAW THE LORD

IN THE BEGINNING

MY NEIGHBORHOOD

SHOW EM'

LOVE LOST LOVE

SOMETHING ADD PRODUCED

I the Son

My Life
Mine

1962

The year after I was born the nation was torn by the

violent death of our president.

Five years passed and we were given the task

of mourning the death of a King.

Past the horizon of my neighborhood tall buildings

stretched as they stood under the watchful eyes of

the sky.

On a planet that spins I'm no bigger than a pin like

a grain of sand on the ocean floor.

But the master was so wise

even though it seems disguised,

to put the burden of its preservation on me.

1962 is when my purpose began. What about you?

My clock is ticking, only time to be true,

God's got me covered until I'm thru.

1

It's not over until I flat line or

see the sign for the finish line.

It may be a different start for you

but for me it was 1962.

God thought enough to see,

in his purpose he saw me

and to fit me into the puzzle of life.

And he thought enough of you

and remained perfectly true

in including you in his master plan.

You're not here by happenstance

or a random act or chance.

He never misses or makes a mistake.

In your small place in time

don't be guilty of the crime

of not knowing your importance to the world.

As I stroll down my street

and people I pass and meet,

the power to change their lives is in my mouth.

One person, two, or three, can only simply be,

the greatest feats of strength in human history.

And some who I don't know,

watch my reactions and my flow

and are changed without even knowing when.

For the simple unseen deeds of sharing life's keys,

to someone who may one day change the world.

1962 is when my purpose began. What about you?

My clock is ticking, only time to be true,

God's got me covered until I'm thru.

It's not over until I flat line,

or see the sign, for the finish line

It may be a different start for you,

but for me it was 1962.

One day I'll stand amazed

as before me a long line looks gazed,

to shake the hands

of the one who changed their life.

I won't remember who they are,

or what simple words were stars

that shined so bright to erase their ignorance.

And as my body lies in dirt impervious to the hurt

of a million people lost of destiny.

The world can rely on the thousands that I tried

to help on my journey from 1962.

1962 is when my purpose began. What about you?

My clock is ticking, only time to be true,

God's got me covered until I'm thru.

It's not over until I flat line,

or see the sign, for the finish line

It may be a different start for you,

but for me it was 1962

The Monster

I liked going on trips. My family going on a trip from home far away. We leav'n early in the morning. My mama wake me up early when it was still dark outside. Me and my sisters carried bags to the big black Buick on the side of the house. My mama was always walking back and forth before a trip, saying she checking on things. One time we got all the way to the highway and had to turn back round. Mama say, "I know I forgot to do something" but she couldn't think of it. You could tell my half-daddy was mad. He tried to hide it behind those thick framed glasses but I could always tell. It was funny 'cause when he got mad his little moustache would twist to the side of his mouth. Didn't matter none though, he always did what mama say do. Mama thought she had left the gas on. She say the house could fill up with gas and blow up the whole block! Now when she say get ready, we taking a trip, I always take one or two of my favorite toys I don't want to get blowed up. One day maybe we can leave my older sister. If she blow up that would be fine.

After we circled the block to give mama time to remember what she think she didn't leave or turn off, we got going on the highway. The lights from the highway were bright but soon it got dark. Every now and then a big green sign would pass us and tell us something. I didn't try to read 'cause it was going too fast and my eyes were heavy. I can read a little but slow. Soon the big buildings and the city was far behind us and I saw the stars brighter than ever. I tried to stay awake but soon my head was jerking down. I kept pullin' it back up to stay woke. I don't remember going to sleep but I did.

I felt the car turn funny. I pushed my eyes open and shut them so the sun wouldn't burn them. I tried it 2 more times and soon was able to keep them open but I squinted. I stretched real hard like a cat and yawned. My sister Steph'nie pushed my face and said, "Dang, you got dragon breath!" My oldest sister Penny laughed but I didn't care. I rub the stuff out my eyes and looked out the window. We were pulling into a rest stop and my half-daddy said we should use the washroom. My oldest sister got out first and Steph'nie ran past her. Half daddy got out slowly and stretched and him and mama laughed about something. They always be laughing bout

7

something but I never know why. Sometimes mama say "Shhh" and they look at me but burst out laughing. Mama tell him, "You should be shame of yourself" and shake her head smiling. When I stepped out of the car something sure was different. The air was different to breath and smelled nice. Then there were the trees! I had never seen so many trees and they were big! I think they made the nice smell. They were green and were everywhere! Mama told half-dad to take me to the washroom with him. He rub my head and said, "C'mon lil man." That's what he called me sometimes, except when he mad. When he mad he call me "Got daggit." He say, "Got daggit, come here" or "Got daggit, didn't I tell you not to leave your toys in the floor"? I don't know what it mean, maybe it from

Afrika or some'thin'. My teacher show us a map and say we come from there. We go to the washroom and come back. My sisters are by the edge of the concrete looking at something in the woods. Mama tells us to come back and half-dad looks at his watch: "It's time to get going." We race to the car.

Mama made lunches and soon we were eating my favorite; Bologna and cheese sandwiches. I unwrap the foil and bite into my warm sandwich. I love the warm baloney and cheese and bite deep into the triangle. Mama hand me some potato chips and a piece of fruit. I do like my sister and put chips in my sandwich and I like the crunch. We laugh and joke, stop at some gas stations and it gets really hot outside. Soon, half-dad say "We are now in the great state of Mississippi!" We sing silly songs and my sisters count the different license plates as we past them. I didn't know we were in a race but mama tell half-dad that, "If he didn't kill us he might win the race." I can see in the middle mirror his mustache twist to the side.

Aunt Tee Tee was standing in the yard when we pulled beside the house. She is round with big cheeks and slanted eyes. She smiling hard and hugs my mama hard. She hugs half-dad but I don't see her smile hard. Her eyes fall to Penny who is the tallest. "Chiile, you don got big….and pretty! I can see yo daddy all in you!" Penny smiles like she crazy! Stephanie grins and buries her pointy chin into aunt Tee Tee's chest. I think I hear her back crack. I'm really little so I hope she don't break my back. "Oooohhhh, who is this handsome man"! She bends down and looks me close in the face. "What's your name baby"? "Darryl", I told her. "Well Darrin, it's so good to see you, there some sweets in the house I bet you would like." My eyes get wide and I smile but I don't move. I'll wait for my mama. Then I here this giant! "Heeeeeyyyyy! How yaw'll doin'?" His name is Unca Benny and he big. He got busy hair that's white and bright green eyes. "Well, I see yaw'll got in." "C'mon in, it's too hot out here!" Unca Benny had big eyes and he was funny. He got a big belly and wears blue jeans up to his shoulders. Unca Benny was right! It was hot! I never felt the sun on my skin like that and I follow him inside. The house is big. We go pass the one room and go through the door to the dining room.

11

My eyes got big again. There are more cakes and pies than the store back home. They all on the table, on the side and even on the big dresser with the pictures on it. Unca Benny say, "Heeey, I see how you lookin' at that chocolate cake, hold on". Unca Benny was right. I looked right past all the other cakes and saw the chocolate one under a glass bowl. It looked sweet and shiny. Unca Benny came back from kitchen with a big smile and a glass of milk. He took the top off the cake and cut a small piece and put it on the plate. "Go head boy," he said with a big smile. Unca Benny's hair was white and with his green eyes he looked like my troll toy. I ate the cake and took some milk to wash it down. It was the best cake I ever had. Half dad laughed at Unca Benny cause mama fussed at him for giving me cake before dinner. I ate fast so it was too late. Later there was so much food and so many people I almost most got lost in the house. The house smelled of fried fish and everybody slopped biscuits in dark syrup and talked loud. A few people was around the TV. They laughed and joked but I could tell there was something else. That night, me and my sisters slept in the same room. I got the little unfolding bed close to the floor. I said my prayers. I don't remember falling asleep. It took a long time though to fall to sleep after I saw a giant water bug fly! I didn't know they could fly!

When I woke up I smelled biscuits and bacon, eggs and grits! My stomach answered by growling. My mama was up but my sister Steph'ne was still slobbing. My oldest sister Penny was already moving. I heard my aunt Tee Tee and my mama and 'Sister' talking loud. Aunt Sister lived next door in the green house with her son Eddie Earl. She was tall and real dark. When she talked her bottom lip and jaw was always full of something. "Girl, your kids don got so big, you better watch them girls, they'll be drawing them boys soon", she said. Then she spit brown stuff in a coffee can. My mama smile and tell her "girl you know, right!"

I don't see Unca Benny. After breakfast I go thru the front room where the TV is. The man on the TV looks worried but tell us not to. He talkin' in front of a big map. I walk through the door unto the front porch. It has screens to keep the bugs out and plenty of plants. My other sister is already outside and tells me to come on. I walk down the brick stairs and see

14

that the house is in the middle of the street but the cars turn both ways to the sides as they come. "Hey come here", my sister says, "lets looks for lizards". "Lizards? I ask, what's a lizard?" "Oh my God, I forgot you are retarded." I told her I was not and that I would tell mama. "Ok, look, they little green creatures, let's catch one!" So now, me and Steph'ne on the side of the house where the bushes are. She say you have to look hard 'cause they can change to the color of whatever they sit on. I see something move and I yell "Steph'nie, I think I see one!" Steph'nie always has a smirk on her face. Most of the time she try to get me in trouble but then I see it again! It's long and green with a long tail and true, it's the same color of the leaf. "Don't just stare at it; grab its tail, unless you scared". I try to be fast and grab for it but it jumped and disappeared into the bushes. "Aw man", I said, he was too quick!" Just as I moved, I barely seen another one. He was a different color, the color of the house. Without thinking I grabbed his tail and pulled him off the side of my Aunt Tee's house. Steph'nie's eyes got big 'cause I surprised her. What happened next sent both of us running in the house. The lizard wiggled hard until his tail came off in my hand! He ran into the bushes by the house. I screamed and threw down the wiggling tail and ran. Steph'ne stopped on the porch and fell out laughing. She probably knew that would happen.

I never seen so many people. My Aunt Tee Tee's house was full of people. Dey were in every room in the house and filling up Aunt Tee Tee's and sister's front yard. Mama said we was having a fam'ly reunion. I asked her what was that and she said that it's when all the families from Hatts'burg come back home. Mama said all of the people coming were family. Dey was an aunt or cousin or unca or something. Then I saw a lady that look just like my mama but short! Then one look like my Aunt Chris! Dey all standing around talking and laughing. Dey even some kids my age. I see two boys that look like me and my mama take me over to introduce us. Dey my cousins. Rodney is kinda chubby with brown eyes and Chucky is taller and darker. We play together and talk about our matchbox cars. I figure I would show them my cars so I pull them out my pocket. I have five that are really cool. Chucky looks at Rodney and smile. Dey pull out a case shaped like a wheel and open it. It's full of a hundred cooler cars than mine. I feel stupid with my 5 cars.

But soon people stop laughing. When me and my cousins come from the backyard I can tell something is different. The man on the radio is saying something. It must be 'portant 'cause everybody start getting quiet. My Unca Frank got a gold tooth 'cept I can't see it no more. Even he look worried. People start leaving. All the men start talking. Something was coming. My Unca Ben shake his head and say he seen it before but this one was gonna to be a monster.

The men work all the rest of day. Dey board up all the windows of Aunt Tee Tee's and Aunt Sista's house next door. It's dark inside of Aunt Tee Tee's house, even in the day. The sun is still shining. All the men in the neighborhood are boarding up the windows. You can hear the banging all day of hammers. I see some people drive from their houses with all dey stuff on it. Are they going a trip too? It's starting to rain. When Unca Benny closes the front door its dark and raining hard. It has just been bright but I guess it get dark fast in Miss'sippi. The trees are blowing a little and you can hear no cars. Soon it sound like rocks hitting the roof and porch: Lots and lots of rocks. Soon the lights go off. A few people made a noise and acted strange when they flickered off for good. You could hear the wind pushing the leaves outside. I was scared so I got under mama. She told me it was going to be alright but I am still scared.

When we got to aunt Tee's and Unca Benny's house there was only me, mom, half-dad, my sisters Penny and Stephanie. Now the house was full with people in every room. Aunt Sister was there and my Unca Nap from Chicago. All the lights were out but there were lanterns and candles. When somebody took the lamp to another room I could see my Unca Nap's cig'rette light up in the dark. I could make out his eyes squinting. He sat listening to the radio with batteries in it. We had one at home in case of 'mergencies. Sometimes I sneak it in the closet and listen to music.

That's when I heard it. That's when I first heard the monster. It came from outside low at first but grew. I could hear it breathing. It howled a low howl and I could hear it pushing the branches of the trees.

Every now and then something would crash outside and everybody would make a sound. The monster was getting closer and stronger. Mama and the rest of the people in the house laid on the floor. "Rooooooaaaaaaaahhhhh, whoooooooooooooosssshhhhhh", all night. My mama and my aunt Tee Tee dem was on the floor and started praying. "Lawyd Jesus protect us….don't let it blow the house down". I prayed and asked Jesus to help us too. Even Unca Frank and half-dad prayed. Just den, the house shook. Some people yelped and screamed. Unca Nap put down his cig'rette and prayed too. I liked Unca Nap 'cause he talked funny and laughed at his own jokes. When he talked to people he got real close and always had a stinky cig'rette blowing cool smoke. He would pull his pants up in the front with his wrist 'cause he was holding his cig'rette. When uncle nap talked nobody else would talk. It must be because he was important. Then, somethin' slammed into the side of the house, wham! Some lady screamed and it seemed like the house was gonna' shake apart. The monster was close and trying to kill us all. I was scared and put my head down. I was sorry I kicked my sister and called her a name. Sunday I didn't put my money in church but bought a coconut bar from outside. It was nasty and I was spittin coconut all day. I could hear the wind swirl loud and the groans and squeaks of the monster. "Oh lawyd, Ka'mill gonna kill us all for sho," some lady said. From someplace close outside I heard the ripping and creaking of something being killed by it. It creaked and cracked so loud I heard it in my head! Crooooaaaaaaaaccccccccckkkkkk! Ka'chack! The sound disappeared past the house. Everybody was praying snd it sound like church. It sounded like the choir singing in their red and white robes with the big letters on it. The preacher would sing and hit the stand he stood behind. It would scare me when he sang his words and beat the table. Den he would take a deep breath after every word like he was having a hard time breathing. "And I, huuuuuhh, just want to say, huuuh, Jesus, huuuh, is allllll you need, huuu…." The house was shaking more and I could hear Kamille getting closer. I don't know why they call him Kamille but I heard Auntie say 'she' was coming in. Most monsters that be in my room when I sleep I thought was a man

23

monster but I don't know. Whatever this was she was shaking the house and causing people to pray. Kamille musta been big cause it sound like something stepped on a car outside. She threw trees against the house and people gasped and stayed on the floor. I grabbed mama lap and looked up from time to time.

"Pass me not oh gentle savior, hear my huuumble cryyy, while on others thou are call iinngg, do…not pass…me by"… I could barely hear it at first. Kamille was so loud throwing trees and stepping on cars, trying to get in but it came soft from the crowd somewhere in the dining room. "Let me at Thy throne of mer…cy… Find…a sweet relief: Kneeling there in deep contrition…help my disbelief"… When she kept singing I started forgetting about the monster. I kept hearing her pretty voice. Seem like it was in my head. Then I look around and seem like ev'body was getting quiet. The next time she started singing….she wasn't alone.

"I'm crying….Saviour….Saviour….hear my hum..ble cryyyy….While on others thou art calling….do…not pass….me…by".

Kamille musta got real made den. She rooaaarrred and cussed and shook the windows trying to get people to gasp and cry. I think the monster was trying to scare us to death but it was too late. Right around the second time singing, Unca Benny started singing. His belly got tight and pushed out deep words that I could feel in my chest. It was deep like the guy on the record my cousins showed me. It was 4 or 5 guys in suits singing bout they girl or something. My cousins told me dey was the guys on the record even though 3 of them didn't look like them. Dey danced and sang to the record like dem so I belied them.

My mama sang high. Mama cried when she sang and I could see her tears on her face a little from the yellow lantern light. Errybody looked serious but continued to sing louder and louder til Kamille start getting scared. She howled like my neighbor's dog getting beat or like the monster dies in the movies at home. My sister all be scared and get under the blanket but peep out when the hero kill him. I hear her a little, being drowned out by the singing. It filled up the house. People start pray'n and thanking God for stuff. Some people say we trust you Lawd.

Some people just kept singing. They sang late. I musta felled asleep. I don't remember when.

When I woke up it was quiet. Unca Nap and Benny opened the door slowly and let the first light in. The sun rays went through the dark room and burned my eyes again. Most went to the front yard. Dey say dey was glad to be alive and God had spared them. The sun was very big in the sky and the sky was real blue like my favorite crayon. The giant tree across the street at Ms. Mabley house was broke and on it side. Some houses were smashed in and trees and telephone lines were in the street. Unca Benny say it wasn't safe to go out til the 'lectric company come out. People in the other houses come out too. Dey was looking around at all the broken stuff but mostly looked glad. I looked around the corner of my Aunt Lucille's house and saw some lizards running. I wonder if the one I pull off his tail was around. The monster was gone, probably someplace else. Probably hoping she find someplace where dey wasn't no fam'ly reunions. She prob'ly go someplace where people what not gon' start praying or singing. Must be someplace else with other kinda people 'cause all my people be praying and singing at church, maybe like my mama be singing around the house.

I took a deep breath. It felt good going in and smelled like rain and flowers. I picked up a branch. It was still wet. The sun was getting hot again. I could feel it on my arm. My Unca Ben with the green eyes was laughing again. Him and Unca Nap and half dad, joked and patted each on dey backs and shook they head as they looked around. I could smell bacon and stuff from the front yard. Auntie dem was at it again. My stomach started acting like Kamille. My cousins started talkin stuff but I didn't care. I punched one and he started laughing. My mama call me to stop but half dad say let em be. We ran around the yard with broken branches playing sword fight. I love my fam'ly. Unca Benny promise to take me fishing next time. For the first time, I could hear the birds chirping. I guess it was they turn to sing.

Hurricane Camille was the second of only 3 category 5 storms to make landfall in the United States in the 20th Century. It sustained winds of 190 miles per hour. Its true speed will never be known since the measuring equipment was destroyed when it made landfall at the mouth of the Mississippi River. It was the first to receive a person's name. The 'Monster' killed 295 people, injured 8,931 and destroyed 5, 662 homes.

It was my 1st family reunion. I was 6 years old.

Rough Love Hands

September 16, 2007

Course hands, work hands

Stroking mine

Keeping me alive

Praying me back with rough hands,

rough love hands.

Sorrowful eyes that see tomorrow

But cried for today,

Worn and deep

Making me turn away

Away from her pain/my pain

Reflected in her eyes.

Meals great meals

Prepared from the heart,

Out of substance

Singing us together, keeping us connected

across a king's table

We ate and laughed, she watched and ate last

Sheltered we were. Poor …never.

Daddy's Tears

Daddy's tears are not like Mama's tears.

His flow from the frustrations of life,

And feeling like he can't win,

Can't ever get over,

Just gettin' by.

Daddy's fears are not like sister's fears.

They come on slowly and don't show

'Till his strength is gone,

And he's old.

Daddy's songs are not like brother's songs.

His speaks more of living

and capturing someone's heart.

Its anticipated hope,

Universal!

Daddy's strengths are not like a man's strength.

He's not a father unless he's working,

puts up with more than he should,

Loves his woman

To death.

Daddy's ending is not like the story's ending.

No regrets.

Admirations and the tipping of hats.

Just a chapter closing really,

Continuing on in his children.

If I was in Charge of My Life

If I was in charge of my life

I would make everything perfect.

The wind would blow in unison with my visions,

And the flowers would bloom year round.

Sweet, bright and pretty

Lining every road taken.

If I was in charge of my life

I would never fail.

I would not bear the scars of unsuccessful attempts,

The bruises of missed marks,

and pain, pain so deep that it caused me to

wake from my sleep and ask God why?

If I was in charge of my life

I would always have money,

More than my imagination could dream to use.

I would lavish it on my wife and indulge my

children's whims,

And make my mother's last days paradise.

I would pay someone to feed the homeless,

And build shelters to help the poor.

If I was in charge of my life

I wouldn't owe anybody anything,

My chest would swell in quiet pride

and bill would be just another name.

And I would laugh at the notion

That poverty would even be possible.

If I was in charge of my life

I could have the time to dream

Or be lazy on an island,

Enjoying the water and world around me,

around me.

If I was in charge of my life

I would miss the beauty of living.

The sweetness of winning contrasted against the

backdrop of losing.

The joy inside of pain,

The peace despite the struggle.

Glory

Glory became a shrinking, smaller woman as she aged. The weight she once bore, although not much, from bearing seven children had since succumbed to age and sensibility. Eating for pleasure or even just to get by, had long been replaced by eating to live better. Whatever the case, she was no longer thirty or fifty or even just seventy. What she lost physically was replaced by patience, practicality and wisdom. So when she received a call from her middle son inviting her to dinner, and after she made the 5-mile drive to pick him up from work (his car was down again), she knew it was more than an invitation to eat. This is how the men in her family seemed to communicate. A picnic or barbecue was a time to relax, act silly and show closeness. A long conversation by phone was usually followed by a loan request and an invite to a Friday dinner, apart from the wife and kids could only mean one thing: something was troubling the water. Johnson men did not often share their problems with their women. They felt that being a man meant they were supposed to shield their women from problems and bear the burdens of life alone. Other men couldn't be trusted and they would certainly feel themselves weak for sharing so they bottled it up until almost too late. Needless to say, the Johnson women lived much longer than the Johnson men.

After some small talk about their day and juggling a few restaurant choices, they settle on the Chinese buffet off of I-94. It was a little out of the way and quite frankly the food was mediocre at best. It was always overly crowded so much so that the owners, probably against the will of some city ordinance, had blocked the exit with tables with the goal of squeezing in a few more patrons. This left a log jam of people at the adjacent entrance trying to get in, some prepaying for their meal, some waiting to be seated, and of course a slow trickle of people exiting through the same small wooden glass paneled doors.

After five or so minutes, they assumed their place around the three buffet tables of starchy fried foods and selected whatever they fancied. Glory limped slowly, picking less than John whose intent was to get his money's worth. They sat across from each other alone amongst the bustling throngs of gorgers.

John ate, distracted from whatever meager conversation they managed to stage. He looked at the overly ethnic décor and wondered if people in Chinese culture still decorated like this. His ignorance also occurred to him. He could not tell if the host was Chinese or Korean, only Asian. He felt sure they were of Chinese descent but in reality he didn't really care. What struck him interesting was the variety of people Chinese food had brought together. There were plenty of blacks, but also the crowd was largely Latino. He heard from behind him a Polish dialect, as well as a few he could not make out. It was a ridiculous train of thought of course; other races must have enjoyed Chinese food as much as his.

He noticed that even though time had been kind to his mother, she had begun to show signs of aging. She sloped unintentionally over in her chair eating slowly her rice and vegetables as her eyes closed and opened slowly. She still worked and the 2:00 a.m. risings all week were taking their toll. Still she managed to eke out a sleepy smile from time to time.

Mothers notice things. More aptly they feel or perceive things. It doesn't matter if the child is four or 42; they know the signs of trouble. They know their girls because they once were girls who watched their mothers and sometimes spent times with their mother's mothers. They knew their sons from raising them of course, but also from watching their fathers; and most of all in the older mothers, from watching their husbands for forty or fifty years. They knew how to make their men happy (or miserable) and grew to understand the enormous load their men sometimes carried: trying to raise a family, trying to stay on the right track with their wives when everything in society says do what you feel. Having to work hard for less than they are worth and then, under the abuse of insecure control freaks that somehow became bosses. And then Most of all, they seem to always be wrong. Wrong because they're black, wrong because you're overweight or too opinionated; paid less because even though they're as knowledgeable as the next guy, he has the degree and automatic respect from the system. They felt the frustration of having more bills than money and the impossible task of keeping up with growing hungry children. Young wives sometimes won't understand that they can't get that new dress or hairstyle this week because he doesn't know how to afford it. He simply doesn't know how to make his paycheck stretch and no one sees the 3:00 a.m. meetings with God. He falls asleep hoping tomorrow the impossible will somehow have taken place. Lesser men run. Some hide in bottles or grass; others find temporary relief in other miserable people; and maybe one or two, from time to time, to put a break in between the pressures of work and the demands of a family, they eat with their mother in a crowded Chinese buffet restaurant off I-94.

"What that taste like?" she asked, sleepily referring to the seafood dish. "It's all right", he said emotionlessly. "Taste all about the same". "Really, she blandly said, maybe I'll get some on the next trip. How was your day?" "It was ok." He fought to keep the water in his eyes. He looked around, made a few comments about his job concerns and tried to move on. He tried to stay true to Johnson men. This is how they communicated. "Let me ask you sumin'. You ever seen this cartoon bout this white guy?" she asked. "I don't know why I stopped on this station to watch it 'cause it was crazy!" His thought train was interrupted by surprise. He knew she hated cartoons and didn't care much for comedies especially modern ones. She loved dramas. The thought of her watching some animated series caught him off guard and intrigued him at the same time. After a few guesses at the title of the show she preceded. "Anyway, this fella, he gets this phone call from a bill collector who tells him his wife's credit card amount was a lot of money. The guy says "What?" And then throws up! I mean not just a little, but everywhere! Gallons of vomit, all over the walls and floor. It was the craziest thing I had ever seen!" she chuckled a little and seemed a little shame for finding humor in something so base and sophomoric. John listened intently now shocked. "Then his daughter called from school, she continued, and said she needed so many thousands of dollars to graduate. Then he began to throw up even harder, all on the ceiling, Lawd it was, I mean everywhere! How could they show such a thing?" she said amidst laughing. The thought of his elderly mother watching this cartoon character throw up was simply unexpectedly too much. He had begun to chuckle and soon could no longer control his laughter. He wasn't sure what was funnier the story or the fact that his frail mother was telling it. She went on in disbelief telling it over and over torturing his former mood into submission. His frustration drained as he cried real tears laughing relentlessness at the thought of this cartoon guy throwing up every time he was confronted with owing money and the fact that she was telling it. He was also surprised that this reserved woman had told him of her break from prudeness.

And so they sat mother and son, in a crowded multiracial Chinese buffet restaurant off of I-94, laughing at an unnamed cartoon characters unstoppable barfings. Him relieved and unstressed, temporarily free, Her laughing slightly with a twinkle in her eye, and the wisdom of a mother.

I the Son

November 2006

I am the son of john carter and no one gives a damn.

I told it to the wind and he laughed a dry whisper of a laugh and I knew I was a fool.

I told my story with short singularity, not having a history, only having a personality because I was a child. A child who was grown but not matured: an empty vase that hadn't been poured into; hadn't been molded or painted. I strained and held my hands on my head and told the wind. I held my head, and yelled, "I am somebody", "I am somebody"! He laughed his dry, dry laugh "I am somebody", he tried to hold it in but he laughed at

the ridiculousness of the statement, "I am...
somebody."

Of course I am somebody, you are somebody, we
are somebody, they are somebody, but who? "Who
the hell am I and why am I here"? I asked him
again, the wind, but he remained silent and I only
heard my echo.

It wouldn't have really mattered but I was the son of
john carter. My eyes were his, but not his vision
because he never poured into me. There are no
marks on my skin where his pen scribbled the
history of his family. The memory of his father and
the mistakes he had made so I wouldn't. A manual
on how not to be afraid: to take destiny by the hair
and drag her to me and that it was alright to cry.

Who the hell am I?

Where are the stories of my fore-fathers? Strong black men who endured the torture of the masters' terrible whip and the merciless southern sun; or of great, great, great grandmothers who survived being raped and having their babies ripped from their arms, only to recover and help someone else raise their children, and sing songs of Zion and smile; carried over by songs of Zion and smiling. Singing and smiling when they hurt. Singing to keep from dying, smiling to stop from dying. What about great uncles and aunts that migrated from small cities with big dreams to huge cities to much hate and low paying jobs to unfair housing and…. What strength! I looked on my chest for the stories but his pen hadn't been there. I needed those stories to give me pride, to make it alright to be me. I needed those stories to help me through, carry me over. So I would know it was alright to have a wide nose and wide thick lips and that I could survive.

I didn't know it was wrong to see a woman as a plaything and to empty out my lust on. I didn't know. My mother tried but she had no pen. john carter had it but didn't write it on my face that they were my sisters until marriage, and to guard their hearts like fragile crystal and to listen.

Man, who am I?

Why was I born? Or allowed to survive? I looked for answers written in my skin but he wouldn't know me to write it in because his father hadn't scribbled in his soul on how to act or how to hold the pen one day. So he ran and hid in life, forgetting, creating other palettes before and after me, leaving them blank and lying to the wind, "I am somebody".

Who the Hell are we?

My head slumped to my chin and I died. I died because I didn't know how to live. I prayed for death with the hope of life. I prayed that if I lived I would be somebody. I no longer cared to impress the wind and then I knew, and hell had nothing to do with it.

I knew because I found a new writer with a bigger pen. He scribed it not only in my mind but in my soul. In my soul he scribed:

I am a person of purpose.

A man of character and ideas.

Even though I make mistakes, have made mistakes, have been called a mistake, it does not define me. Uncompromising ideas because they are bigger than me: They did not come from me. They did not come from john carter. They did not come from my mother. I love her so, but she had no pen. Ideas that caused me to stand alone at times but upright; Tired sometimes and often ridiculed but uncompromising ideas.

When I said that the wind took notice

I am a man of principles.

Not for piety sake, but to save me from the destruction of my mind and arrogance. Let God judge me if I am arrogant.

Principles that caused me to be poor at times, but rich; hurt sometimes, but stronger; attacked at times, but prosperous; alone a few times, but at peace; last, but the leader; hated, but admired; attacked, but standing tall.

I am a father.

Not just of the three that come from my blood, but the thousands he, my step-father told me to pour into. Thousands over a lifetime, millions in the future. I didn't know this was in me, but his pen is strong. His words he wrote in the crevasses in my mind were before time; this time for such a time. They notice me, my children, or the words and I write on them to live. I write on them to live and shine. They see the pen and beg to be written on, so I introduce them to my father and I write and pour into them. My days are long, but my hand never tires of writing and pouring because without it, they are lost and dead, written off by the wind, laughed at in secret by its gusts, imprisoned by ignorance and the hopelessness in its bliss. The fury that follows and the folly that fools them into feeling like they are alive.

Who am I?

I am a person on a mission with a small, small window of time, maybe 50 or 60 or 75 or more years to complete. My days don't always make sense and my nights are sometimes long, soaked with my tears praying for answers but my purpose is clear. I am complete in joy because I operate in my purpose. My job is my life's work, my work is my purpose and every day I yield a little more of myself, so that I can prosper, have joy and peace.

Tueseve

Some evenings, but not often, I manage to find some time to myself. Don't get me wrong, I love my family, my job, and the work I do for my church, but I figured out something in the last few years. Everyone needs time to themselves; A completely wasteful moment where you just sit in a park feeling the warm breeze playing the leaves, and the sun, sending its final rays as it escapes to bless another country. Maybe you lie in deep green grass or sit on a secluded bench reading a book. Nothing deep, nothing self-help or scholarly, just that book. The one that's good, but you only pick it up every once in a while like cheesecake. You never finish it because of time. It's not a great novel so you notice when something special happens. You look over the top of its dog eared pages and delight in the orange sparkle on the water as the sun goes to sleep, or a young couple walking aimlessly without talking much. Without touching much, except for their brown hands gently locked, and eyes searching. They are impervious that there is a world beyond each other's shoulders. Maybe you stroll slowly on a downtown street that stretches its legs out with its hands behind its head, relaxed after a hot busy day. Not as bright, but lit with the glow of neon, and a few cars and buses decorating the street. You walk in the tepid evening air, pass closed stores and side walk cafes with the faint smell of coffee and cinnamon, feeling the distant sound of jazz by a street musician who plays not for money but out of sheer enjoyment. It doesn't matter what you do, as long as you follow the rules. It shouldn't cost you much. It shouldn't require much thought. And you should feel somewhat replenished. The idea is to take time for yourself. If you are a selfish person that never gives to anyone else, never sacrifices or puts yourself last, then this won't make sense. It's the contrast that makes it special.

In the winter months, on my mid-week day off, sometimes I would go to the movies alone. My wife would usually be at school and my children on their way to bed. Being around people all the time makes it easy to sneak out south and see a movie solo. I would sit in the dark and try not to think about kids, the job, the future, the room I have to paint, the bills, or the people I serve. I'd mindlessly focus on whatever images are being sent my way while I reclined, scrunched down in my seat, ball cap pulled down close to my eyes while cradling a bag of popcorn and drink way too big for my appetite. The problem came when I realized I had seen most of the movies playing and I was too late for the one I thought appealed to me. I was probably tired of the show anyway and looking for a way to escape what had become routine and boring. Besides, there were only so many good movies released in the winter and I was already scraping the barrel. Although I liked to sit in the café of the local bookstore reading magazines and sipping over-priced lattes, it was too far and my time too limited for the trip. I was a little hungry and somehow got the idea to go to the mall. Now I hated the mall with a passion, but I liked the

Chinese restaurant (for lack of a better word) in the food court. Somehow I made myself believe that I could sit and eat alone, satisfying my scientific mind by watching the dozens of people who strolled past, oblivious to my research. I loved people. I loved to watch people and took note of the amazing differences in them, and the profound similarities. They were short or thick, tall or loud, each showing me a little piece of their world as if actors on the silver screen. I saw teenage girls giggle as they talked about the most important nothings on their planet. They walked back and forth in their little outfits, clad with cell phones and $200 dollar purses. Young men strolled with the latest clothes and slogans trying to sell 'I'm it' to themselves and anyone with the right equipment. I laughed to myself when the mother of one of these young coolios fusses at him for making her exercise all over the mall searching for him. His homies don't even smirk, for fear of residual embarrassment. The giggling girls face each other and explode with laughter. I hoped to myself they didn't go to the same school. Then there were the lone ones. Walking nowhere slow, as if hoping to be discovered. They seem happy, successful, and beautiful, but past the makeup and the nice clothes I see a twinge of escaping hurt; hurt that they believed hidden. They hide it behind attitude and swagger, but nonetheless it's there; hiding amongst the shadows of what could have been, regret, and perhaps loneliness. I want to help but because it is Tuesday evening, I am only an observer. Then there are the mall workers or custodians. Always middle aged, always unnoticed and likely unappreciated. I try to imagine what all these lives that pass my way must have had to go through to pass by my window at this time. I can almost read their stories on their faces, and in the way they walk and interact.

The food court was vast, with the outer wall being lined on three sides with small fast-food openings. People sat in groups of two, maybe three, conversing. At first, I almost didn't see him. He stood probably about 4 feet tall, with short black hair, slanted dark brown eyes, and had wide shoulders topping his thin frame. His clothes were clean, but not new, and had that well-preserved hand me down look. He stood about 15 feet from me and slightly to the right. I didn't see him because I was busy observing far behind him at the mouth of the food court where the main traffic converged. He was out of focus until I looked near and down, and his small thin frame had blended with the pole that stood almost directly behind him. His eyes were soft and familiar. I thought I knew him from church or one of the summer day camp jobs I coordinated. I knew I probably knew him and as he became aware of my attention, he raised his arm only at the elbow and shook his hand from side to side. I smiled and waved back. I loved kids but I was aware of the times. You had to be careful of talking to other people's kids. Parents were distrustful of strangers. I thought it ok to speak, but I looked around to make sure I carefully acknowledged the mother. I panned to the right and saw a Mexican family who probably didn't have a black child. To my left were several people, two guys were talking, an older white man, and just to the left, in the fore ground was a woman, about thirtyish. She was busy attending to a baby in a stroller and seemed oblivious to her older boy. When she finally looked up she politely smiled a smile of approval. The boy had somehow managed to move closer and I saw for the first time that he appeared to be about 10, a year or two older than my middle daughter. "Hi, what's your name" I asked? He looked at me blankly not afraid but with a subtle wonderment. A kind of resolve that someone had finally noticed him. He never looked at his mom but I made sure I did, checking to make sure of any revoking of permission. He didn't answer me. His eyes, soft and compelling as they were didn't hint one way or the other whether he even understood me. It occurred to me that he might be deaf, so I spoke slightly louder over pronouncing the words. Never taking his eyes off of me, he peeked a slight smirk and said "D.J.". For some reason, I thought of my wife's brother's son who was older but looked a little like this boy when he was a kid. We all came up together and me and my brother in law favored slightly as children. Before I picked up the weight and my wife started having babies, people often commented on us looking alike. Something you really don't want to hear when you are young and in love, and you have never met your father. My nephew's J was for junior. He continued to stand a few feet from me but said nothing. I was finished with my meal and cautiously spoke to the child, still mindful of the times. "How old are you D.J.?" "Uhm, ahm ten", he said in a low childlike voice. "Today is my birthday". It was ten days into February and definitely not spring. I said "really", trying to sound excited "how old are you really, 25? 27? 30?" With that he chuckled and showed more emotion than he had shown in the 10 or so minutes he had been watching me, moving his head slightly back while grinning profusely. "Naw man, I'm only ten", he said still chuckling, with a typical boys voice, devoid of bass. "Well D.J., what do you want to be when you grow up?" I thought I detected a moment, and I mean just a moment of sadness, but then he erased it by smiling politely and saying maybe an

69

artist or play an instrument." I would have liked to play the sax but it seems like it got too many buttons to learn". Well this was right up my alley since I was a former saxophonist. Occasionally, I thought back to how I felt the day I had to choose an instrument in band. I remember thinking I would never learn all the switches and levers. My mom had tried to play tenor sax and my wife played alto until she graduated from high school. "It's not that hard, it just takes a little time and work, you'll do fine", I said confidently. "I bet you're pretty good", he remarked. "I was ok back in the day, but I don't really play much now." "Does your mother play", I asked? For the first time he showed his sadness. The questioned seemed to take him by surprise. It was as if another sadder boy had taken his place. When he

70

told me he hadn't seen his mother since he was a baby, my eyebrows quickly raised. "What?" I asked, hoping I heard wrong. I looked confusingly at the mother who had finished bundling up her baby in the stroller preparing to leave. There was a moment of puzzlement as I sorted through the people trying to match him with a suitable mom. It then occurred to me that he probably just didn't have one. Maybe he was unfortunately one of the dozens of kids I come across from time to time whose mom is locked up or worse dead, ravaged by drugs or the harshness of the city streets. I felt bad for the boy but he seemed to have adjusted. Before I could ask him another question he added, "I ain't never seen my older and younger sister either, or my baby brother". Maybe he was a foster child.

Another child, by no fault of their own, locked in a system whose record was strewn with failure and hopelessness. His sadness became mine and it showed in my eyes. I struggled to reign in my compassion, or at best not to show my empathy. Although he seemed all right, I felt compelled to say something encouraging. I searched for something to say, but was in awe by this child's forwardness and his willingness to talk to a complete stranger. He reminded me of some of the kids I counseled, who after going through so much pain and suffering, that they had the resolve of accepting their loss and filing it under 'life'. Ten was a little out of my experience range. I mostly dealt with teenagers but I managed to say a few encouraging words that in the end, seemed more for my benefit. As I finished, he smiled politely and said, "Well I did get a chance to meet my dad." In all my searching it never occurred to look for a man. I was filled with even more dread as a flash of heat streaked across my brain. I thought what if some father sees me talking to his kid and reacts wrongly. I looked behind me expecting to see a 6'3'' 250lb man walking towards me with that look in his eyes. To my surprise there was nobody behind. As I scanned to my left and right I realized that with the exception of a few custodians quickly cleaning before going home, mostly everyone, including the woman with baby, had begun their trek to the main doors, disappearing down the many corridors. I felt a strange sensation come over me. It seemed to take over my body, making me turn in the direction of the boy. He was gone. I got up slowly. My eyes quickly periscope over the sea of tables. I scanned in every direction trying to catch a glimpse of him. I walked briskly around the fake trees and camouflaged garbage cans, hoping I would see him leaving with a parent or guardian. "Lose sumthin?" asked a stout, older janitor. I was so focused on the kid that he startled me. "Uh, did you see a boy? 'bout this high, I was just talking to him". I must have seemed kind of confused to him. "No, but I could call security to help you look for him, is he your kid"? He asked. I stammered, "No, no, I was talking to him but when I turned around he was gone". "Well", he reasoned, "maybe he saw his dad and left".

I walked to my car fighting the cold winter winds, trying to put the episode behind me. Looking occasionally around, I was hoping I would see him and an adult getting into a car. I gave up after a few looks as I got in my Jeep. What really bothered me is how he completely disappeared. While I drove, my feelings slowly shifted to an overwhelming urge to be home with my family, especially my kids. I thought about my son, now six and how I was fortunate to finally have one after four pregnancies. I thought about how blessed I was to have beautiful daughters, eight and 13. They were of course sleep when I came in. Someone had left the TV on so I quietly pushed the button and heard the dulled pop of electricity as the screen went dark. I pulled off my coat and hung it up in the hall closet. On the top shelf I noticed a shiny burgundy binder. Feeling grateful and nostalgic, I pulled the tattered picture album off the shelf, careful not to spill the excess of accumulated pictures. I sat in the kitchen that overlooked my son's bedroom, looking and occasionally smiling at the images of my young family. First walks, first days of school, birthday parties, all frozen in time and chronologically cataloged. We had been through a lot but seeing how much we had changed made me think of how blessed I was. I thought about the boy in the mall. I became increasingly thankful for my small life. Even though we had our problems, as most families do, we had been spared the horrors that life suddenly can bring. I looked until I was overwhelmed. I held back the tears for as long as I could until I felt a sudden rush of silliness. Why and who was I hiding my tears from? My kids were sleep and if they did wake and look out of their rooms into the dimly lit kitchen, maybe it would be good for them to see me crying over old photos. Maybe they would see and understand what's really important in life; love, family, and God. As I pondered, this one photo seemed to lasso my attention. It stood out. I took it from beneath its yellowing plastic shield to get a better look. It was an old picture of my wife. The picture was taken outside in a park. My oldest daughter was sitting across from me on a picnic table, chubby cheeks and all, while her mother held her. The photo stood out because it did not fit the theme of the dozens of typically happy pictures that people normally take and store. No one wants to remember bad times. My wife's face was sad and withdrawn. Her eyes were swollen from crying and her demeanor was as gray as the park on that mild winter day. I stared at it for minutes, focusing in on her eyes. They were dark and sullen and seemed to want to tell a story. I pushed past the walls in my mind to remember why, when it hit me.

Although the picture didn't show it my wife was pregnant. She worried constantly and soon fell into depression. Being young, I didn't know how serious it was. Since I worked a lot, I did not know she had not been sleeping much or eating. We had moved into the suburbs, far from her family. She had the added strain of chasing a two year old. I thought a walk in the neighborhood park would cheer her up.

The date stamped on the back of the photo read February 9th. Ten years and one day ago. The next day she went into the hospital and the baby was still born. Sometime later, I don't remember when, I found out it was a boy. My first son. I have often wondered what he would have been like, or what having another son would have meant. Being younger and less humble, I probably would have named him after myself, Darryl Vincent Smith Jr. His family and friends would have probably called him D.J.

I Saw The Lord

We See Sin

We see sin,

We run in.

Never count cost,

Until we lost.

Feel much pain,

Make us lame.

Find again rope,

Give us hope.

Get back strong

After so long

We see sin…

Run in again.

Eve's Prison

I was only twelve when I first saw her. At least in my mind and in my prayers, she was there clear as day; dark and thick, quiet like the sea, with waves of curves, in places I only heard about and hinted at in songs. I saw her before she saw me, and I felt like Adam. Knew what he must have felt after the mist settled, revealing her, appreciating the ache in his chest. Her smile talked to me; committed to only me, mine for the moment. She seemed to beckon for me, for my soul. Her dark eyes changing with every day's thought. Her dimensions morphing, growing, her body tight and young, mature and sensuous, moving in all the ways that catch my mind, in ways I had not learned.

When I first saw her she was lounging in the grass, seeming relaxed and waiting; Waiting for me to pick her up, to caress her, to take her into my confidence. I felt a twinge of shame. I looked around to see if I was seen, jaws dropped next to other potential slaves as we bumped shoulders, wide-eyed and speechless, each claiming her as our own.

My playground was huge and she seemed so happy and willing. I began to search for her daily, looking in the grass, behind bushes. Then I saw her at the magazine store. I pretended to search for comics, but in truth I had graduated; willing to be satisfied with a simple glimpse (starting to lie to myself); envious of the successful men who had her, wishing it were me.

I managed to see her from time to time over the years. She always presented herself the same; erotic and enticing, blinded to the deadness behind her eyes. She became a forbidden lover, and I enthralled by the intensity of it all; by the danger of it all. Since I could not have her, I began to see every woman as her. I began to see girls who had pieces of her, willing to be her; anesthetizing their pain, yearning for power and/or control. I felt her gentle tug pulling me in, pulling me down; never seeing the plan. Never seeing that behind those smoldering eyes, that fake smile of ecstasy, the shackles she wore.

It took blood and death to see what she was and to break free. I see her now as my lost sister; someone's daughter, and someone's mother. Someone, more than anything, in need of freedom. I feel her pain now, and sometimes I feel remorse that at one point I contributed, if even indirectly, to her slavery.

Tests and Trust

August 14, 2006

What do you do when the bottom drops out?

Do you spiral into oblivion?

Do you curse the day?

The moment you were born to spare yourself the

agony?

Do you curse the day?

Do you wish for the bliss of non-existence?

Does your heart become vulnerable to diversion?

Temporary peace in careful, pretty packages

Filled with love in need of love.

What do you do when the bottom drops out?

When all you know is now backwards.

When all you feel is strange, foreign ground.

The sky is just as blue, but not as sweet.

When right is tired,

And wrong's scent you want to breathe in.

Inhale deep, long and relieving.

What do you do when the bottom drops out?

And you float alone.

Trying to stand on clouds of principles and words,

But alone.

All the time,

With the ache of disappointment and swirls of

confusion.

What do you do?

Is there enough left to hope?

Is there time enough to heal?

Is there healing enough in time?

Are there tears enough for God?

I Saw the Lord

As preached by the late Rev. Theopolous Jones

Moanin' Saints, friends an visitors. Thank you Sista
More for that beautiful rendition. God truly used
you today, amen, amen. Sittin' dare lis'nen made
my mind go back. Made me think about how good
God really is, and how we really don't deserve what
he done. I had a sermon prepared. I did study all
week, prayed, and fasted but I believe God wants
me to go another way dis moanin' and I has to be
obedient. I have listen to y'all over da years tell yo
story, now I'z got to tell my story. How I came to
know him, when I'z first saw him. Is that all right?

Go head Rev., tell it!

Sin ain't neva been prejudice. It will take you where you didn't want to go; take you further than you expected, keep you longa than you wanted to stay, and cost you more than you were willing to pay, and I was full of it.

My mother had always said my head was as hard as a ton a bricks and she was right. I'd stopped going to church soon as I was outta huh house. Not that it held me back none. I probably did just as much devilment in the church basement than most folks do at the juke joint. So God didn't come to me like some folks says; Talkin' bout dey felt His love and His spirit called to them, and dey heard music from on high. Dats fine an dandy, but like I say dat wasn't how he called me. Some of you act like you don't know what I'm talkin' bout but you know what I'm sayin' cause it was dat way for you too!

"You Right Rev. You right, AAAyman!"

I'm glad dat God loves fools and commended His love towards me, yet…. While I was still in my sin. While I was filthy, dirty, and smelly He still loved me. Even when I was graduating in my sins….now dats real love.

When I saw the Lord, I was walking home from sinning. Whiskey yet still on my breath, the scent of perfume on my clothes, late and quite. I had done all I'z said I was gonna do, had accomplished every goal for that evening, had fun and conquered every taboo, but still something was missin'. As I walked through the park, the park was safe to walk in back den you know. I heard His voice really for the first time. Not so much as words but a troublin' kinda sound. I felt a troublin' in my spirit dat I never felt before. It was like da voices of many waters, or the rumblin of the earth. Troublin' me, stoppin' me. I, I, I tried to clear my mind by smoking, but my hands was shakin' too bad to even light up. I looked around for help, but help was not to be found. My heart began to beat out of my chess, I began to sweat and tremble. I thought, this must be da end.

"Uh-huh, go head preach now!"

Just when I thought it was over, it plum got worse. He began to bring cross my mind like a movie all da sins I had been doin'. All da drinkin', an da cussin'; all da lyin', all da hoeing right dare before my eyes. I saw the peoples I hurt. The womens who was left

94

broken and shame. I'z saw for the first time all the people I let down. I'z saw my mama crying and a weeping on huh knees pleading for my sorry self. Den it occurred to my mind how much God must have been disappointed. All those years of callin' me. Saving me from danger, givin' me chance afta chance and for what? For me to spit in His face! That's what you do you know, when you reject Him, you spit in His face!

"Aww Man preacha, you know you right!"

That's when the truth hit me. It hit me like a ton a cement. Like a train fulla steam. Like the bullet from a gun. I was on my way to hell and it was gonna be dat night!

"Look out now preacha! Tell the truth!"

I fell to my knees, knowin' my fate, knowin' my destiny. I thought about all the things I coulda done, all da things I coulda' ben, all the things dat coulda made my mama proud, but now it was too late. As I lay on the dew wet grass, head spinning, chest a poundin', all I could do was to say I was sorry. Not a fake sorry dat just come from my lips just because I was caught, but sorry from my heart. I felt da sadness of the wrongs of my actions, the waste of my life. So you know what I did?

"What you do Rev.! Tell it right!"

I called out his name, JESUS! HAVE MERCY ON ME! You know you can call on his name don't you. You know no matta the situation, no matta how low you sunk, as long as the breath in your lungs and the blood runnin' warm in yo vains, you can call on His name!

When I called Him, sumthin' happened. I looked up to the sky and I saw Him plain as day.

"Preach, Preacha'!"

When I saw the Lord He was High and lifted up. He was clothed in Righteousness. Hisa hair was a like the storm clouds and across His chest was a banner that said "Holy, Holy, Holy."

"Tell da truth preacha'!"

When I saw the Lord, in one hand were lightnin' and thunder, and in the other was His Grace. He held out his hands and spoke. So loud in my mind dat it shoulda woke da dead. So loud dat time stood still. So loud I don't know if I was livin' or dead or in-between. His voice was like the rolling of the thunda. His voice was like the cheering of the billions of saints throughout the ages. His voice was like da smashing of a mountain as He said to me "CHOOSE YE THIS DAY WHO YOU WILL SERVE".

I like dat Rev.Preach!

I fell to my face and lay prostrate before him. He was too holy to look apon. I tried to speak with my mouth but nothing came out. Just then two angels and two cheribums were dispatched from outta' His glory, and dey said "God don't hear from your lips, God only listen's to a sorry heart".

"You preaching now doctor, preach!"

I said with a broken heart, I said with a bowed down spirit Fatha, I stretch my hand to thee, I need you like a fish needs da water, like the clouds need da sky, and like a child needs a motha'. Help yo poor child, please suh. Have mercy on me ah sinna, ah wretch undone. I don't deserve yo love. I don't deserve yo peace. I don't deserve yo presence now, but if you in da mood for passing out mercy, please don't forget about me!

"Whoooowee! Thank ya!"

Then he said to me, son it will be all right. I began to feel the weight lifting off my shoulders and chest. Like I had been pinned by a mountain. I felt the heaviness leave my mind.

That night I saw the lord, I felt wave afta wave of His love floodin' my soul, chasing away the darkness in my mind. With tear soaked eyes (you know I cried don't you?). Like a lost child dats found its mama.), I was so grateful I promised to serve him all the days of my nat'rl life. Promised not to waste a minute mo' eating from da devils table. And with dat, He was gone.

"Halleluiah! Praise Him!"

Dats my story but it's not enough. You got to see Him fo' yoself. You got to know him fo yoself. You can't ride on yo mama's coat tail. I don't care if yo daddy was a preacha', you got to call on Him like everyone else dat wonts to be his child.

"Dats tight but its right preacha'!"

Now dats da way it was for me, dats da way it is, and dats all I'm gon say bout it.

Sista mo, sang!

Your voice in me

I say I'm trying,

And you say I'm free.

I say I'm hurting,

But you say I'm healed.

It hinders when I confess feelings that's contrary

to your word.

And change occurs when I start listening

to the truth I've grown to know.

I get delivered,

And I get free.

I get healed,

And I can see.

Then the world's not as cold,

And the road not so hard.

When I really listen,

what I really hear…

is your word in me

Your voice in me!!!

It's not that you're silent,

When I'm filled with tears.

You speak soft and strong,

Straight through my fears.

But sometimes I forget,

or make up in my mind,

that someway I can handle it

But only when I break down.

I get delivered,

And I get free.

I get healed,

And I can see.

Then the world's not as cold,

and the road not so hard.

When I really listen,

What I really hear

Is your word in me.

Your voice in me!!!

Calm me tenderly.

Renew my strength in you.

Straighten out my heart,

So I can live again.

So fragile is my mind,

I have to concentrate on you.

All the time I'm living

so I can remain....

Delivered,

and free indeed.

Healed,

and continue to see.

Then the world's not as cold,

and the road not so hard.

Because I really listen,

What I really hear is your word in me.

Your voice in me!!!

The Lazy Hazy Sun

The lazy hazy sun hung over our heads,

or so it was said.

The lazy hazy sun hung over our heads.

The lazy hazy sun hung over our heads, a bright

blood red or so it was said.

The lazy hazy sun hung over our heads.

The lazy hazy sun hung over our heads, a bright

blood red real close to bed.

The lazy hazy sun hung over our heads.

The lazy hazy sun hung over our heads, a bright

blood red real close to bed, our dreams it fed.

The lazy hazy sun hung over our heads.

The lazy hazy sun hung over our heads, a bright

blood red real close to bed,

our dreams it fed, washing our heads.

The lazy hazy sun hung over our heads.

The lazy hazy sun hung over our heads, a bright

blood red real close to bed,

our dreams it fed, while washing our heads,

for sins it bled.

The lazy hazy sun hung over our heads.

The lazy hazy sun hung over our heads, a bright

blood red real close to bed,

our dreams it fed, while washing our heads, for sins

it bled…the story read.

The lazy hazy sun hung over our heads.

Her Two hearts

August 8, 2009

Two hours after sunrise she awoke. Her eyes strained to open and first rebelled against the order. The light, no matter how diluted from the average beige drapes, stabbed her pupils mercilessly and without pity. They cracked and shut suddenly, cracked and shut suddenly, then gradually strained, and accepted the change. The next 30 minutes were attempts to stave off the start of another day. She tried to go back to sleep, but having tasted consciousness, her mind raced with a montage of important tasks. It eventually marionetted her body to the side of the bed; dragged her for a grateful stoop at the toilet; and soon made her the benefactor of the gentle slap of too hot water.

Her reflection in the steamed mirror was kind. It ignored her thick messy hair, her tired demeanor and makeup free face. They were all overshadowed, and paroled by her eyes. Her eyes were deep and brown and beautifully haunting. She didn't believe the mirror, and doubted that at this early in the morning, and at her age, she was who it said she was; a 40 year old lovely woman with a great shape and deep brown hauntingly beautiful eyes.

This was her normal routine.

With her checklist in mind, she went about her day. She sipped her coffee, unsatisfied because it wasn't from the Burger joint. She made a few calls, and watched the local news and the flurry of negative happenings in her community. Mostly though, she used it as a backdrop of sound as she checked her emails, and texts; and went over which bills would get paid; how much, and which ones would be a sacrifice to the struggle.

She had not worked in weeks, and began to feel the effects slowly as the month flew by. It was by no choice of her own, but that of a nervous cautious boss. She shared with him her issues with her legs and feet. They had begun to swell suddenly, making it difficult for her to stand and move normally. She wasn't sharing to get out of work, but to explain her lack of energy; and because she thought he was more than a boss, but also a friend. It proved to be a mistake. Citing liability over anything else, she was told she needed a bill of good health to return. She left that day feeling dumb and betrayed, but sucked it up and tucked it away. Her life had always had challenges. She would suck it up and do what she had to do.

Patrice was a woman of great faith and meager resources. She worked hard on finishing college, even though she was interrupted at times. She enjoyed serving at church diligently when asked. She had a great sense of herself, her mission; and had managed to focus through the noise in her life over the years. She was a survivor; a mountain climber, even thought it didn't reap the benefit of news coverage, or a parade or money. She did so to please God, who made sense of her life.

So a few weeks ago when she went to the clinic because of her feet, she automatically geared for battle. Bad experiences with doctors and hospitals left her mistrustful, and she initially masked her fears with excuses on why she should not go. However, at the urging of friends she kept her appointments, and painstakingly made it through the tedious conundrum of tests. Having no real insurance, she easily fell prey to discouragement by the culture of bureaucracy that surrounds the almost poor. But as her condition worsened and she became less able to heal herself, she succumbed to and submitted to a battery of test that pointed to a potential problem with her heart.

She was brave, but could feel the fear lurking in the corner of her mind. It was small and dangerous, but submitted to her bravery and faith, so it lacked the strength to grow. She smelled it from time to time, and exorcised it from her thoughts. She knew it was not gone for good, so she guarded her heart from those who would feed it by worrying and overreacting. She would not tell this group, especially her mother. Geared up with her mp3 player and purse, she locked the door, caught the elevator down, and marched, inspired on to the street to a song booming in her headphones. It was a lost song to her that hadn't been heard in ages, and its rhythm and message appeared timely. Patrice walked gingerly, being a little sore, and prayed she would not miss the bus. After 10 long minutes, she stood on the corner, and after a while she realized she was not alone. Her music hid the arrival of a woman 20 years her senior. She was probably tall like her, possessing a similar build with ridiculously big, dark sunglasses. She could not tell if she was looking at her and so she did not speak. If the woman spoke, she would not have heard her for the concert booming in her ears. She sat atop an expensive looking electric wheelchair. Strapped on the back like a canteen, was a small oxygen tank. From its top crept a double clear plastic tube that ran up her back and across her face and nose. The woman seemed strangely familiar to her, although she was certain they had never met. She imagined that once upon a time the woman was very beautiful, and she pondered the set of events that caused her to be in her current state. Patrice felt the fear attempt resurgence, but shook it from her thoughts quickly. The bus timed its stumble down the street perfectly. It extended its flat metallic spatula, and noisily lifted the wheelchair lady into its side. It happily took Patrice's money and continued on its northerly journey.

She sat quietly near the rear. The front represented the old folks section and the wheel chair took half of that up. She amused herself slightly when she noticed how everybody's head bobbed and jerked in concert, conducted by the sudden stop and go of the bus and the city potholes. A pop song from the 90's seemed to synergize the whole phenomenon into a video, making it even harder not to giggle. It was a silly thought, but it took her mind off the meeting ahead. She fought back a smile and tried to think of something else, less she be considered one of the strange people on the bus by the kids, as she had also judged so many years ago.

What if she has a heart condition? What if the test was negative and she needed a new heart? The donor list for heart replacements was extensive and she had no formal insurance. If it was, her activities would be curbed and her friends and family would drive her crazy. As her health worsened, she would not be able to walk and most assuredly would need an oxygen tank. Her eyes would discolor and...she suddenly realized she was in a day-mare. Fear had not only left the corner of her mind but now took residency on the seat next to her! She cursed herself, repented and angrily righted her thoughts by telling herself she was better than that for slipping. She tried to find solace in the bobbin bus heads but the moment had passed. She scrolled her Mp3 player and settled on her favorite gospel song to encourage herself.

"In life it doesn't matter what may come...

The problems of our lives seem to overtake some....

Although I trust in His sovereignty and not what I feel....

I believe by faith, it's His will to heal..."

He didn't go back to his corner easily, having stretched his legs but slowly, he angrily submitted.

The clinic was a who's who of third world faces and thick heavy accents. She checked in and took her seat in the overly crowded waiting area. She wanted to continue listening to her songs but thought she would miss hearing her name being called. The large woman at the station spoke just above her speaking voice. It was irritating and took great concentration to hear her call names with such indifference. The air was already full; with a sea of languages, two competing televisions and interoffice paging. Patrice thought to herself that the woman just didn't care. It would cause her to snap if she had to wait longer than necessary because someone whose job it was to perform such a simple and mundane task, refused to elevate her voice a couple decibels. Thirty minutes after checking in, an hour and a half after leaving her house and six hours after the sun rose, she sat waiting to hear the results of a heart test, and learn if her life was about to be interrupted in the worse way. She sat frozen, with only her thoughts, her future in the hands of God.

Dr. Chinn sat across from her fumbling through a couple of files. Her first impression of the doctor was that of wondering just how young she really was. She looked all of twenty three, but that wasn't likely unless she was a child genius. On her previous visits she'd searched for a diploma or something on the wall that could verify her age and calm her down. Even if she had a diploma, she reeked of newness and inexperience. Besides, if she was a genius, she would not be at the free clinic on south water street. Patrice tried to remain open but now questioned everything the doctor said. Every test she ran, every decision she made for another test to eliminate the possibilities was scrutinized. At one point the young doctor looked through a medical journal in front of her. Patrice noted to herself that she had first tried, but gone against her mindset of researching on the internet and healing herself to avoid doctors. She left frustrated. It took a while but after some strong-arming by her friends, she submitted herself to whatever the doctor came up with, within reason. Her blood work and symptoms pointed to something possibly wrong with her heart. Two weeks later she was sent to a specialist at the hospital on the north side where they injected her with dye and took pictures of her heart. She tried to read the faces of the technicians for the results, but they were too practiced at their craft.

After drawing out an unnecessary greeting, she pulled out the results of the test. "Well, I'm glad we ordered this particular test." She spoke in an almost childlike voice. "I wanted to confirm my previous findings." With that, there was a knock at the door. A tall black nurse asked the doctor to step out into the hall. She apologized with a smile an excused herself from the room. If there was a worse time to be interrupted or to take a break, she couldn't imagine it. She tried not to think but could not focus over the silence of the room. She thought about her song and tried to say the lyrics, but succumbed to thoughts of her father who died when she was a child. They say it was likely his heart. She felt and battled the hot rush of tears just behind her eyes. They sat poised to invade her face but were held back by a crumbling levy of grit and determination. The doctor returned. Patrice could feel her heart beating so hard she wondered if it could be seen beating through her blouse. The doctor resumed where she left off and said the tests were all negative and her heart was strong and healthy. She explained that what she did suffer from was a deficiency of a certain protein and that it was the cause of her symptoms. Medication would correct the problem. Patrice thanked the good doctor. She barely cleared the clinic grounds when the levy broke. These tears were not the same ones as before. These were conceived of relief and peace, joy and a grateful heart. They invaded her face and lifted the weights off her shoulders.

Trusting in the Real

A Song of hope

Looking out of my window

Through eyes that have been redeemed.

The world appears much different than before

Or maybe it's me that's changed.

But I still carry the load

Of my father's generations.

From time to time I feel a little low.

And it feels so real.

The hope I've found is real.

It's carried me through.

What else can I do?

It's just so real.

'Cause it seems so real,

The peace I've found is so real.

I've been put in a place

Only to trust.

To trust in the Real.

It's amazing what time can do.

Makes you wait until you're mature.

Only then do you appreciate

What God saw from afar.

That every problem you have faced,

Every event you went through,

Was allowed to happen

To shape who you are today.

And He feels so real.

The hope I've found is real.

It's carried me through

What else can I do?

It's just so real.

'Cause it seems so real.

The peace I've found is so real.

I've been put in a place

Only to trust,

To trust in the Real.

Soul oil

One day while in the shower,

much less than an hour.

I felt a foreign substance,

come from my chest, and then I said,

"What is the stuff that comes from me;

From my chest what could it be"?

Immediately I was on the phone.

And the doctor hearing the panic in my tone,

Said "calm down, get dressed, come see me now

I think I know what, why and how.

I was hyper of course as I sprinted to my car,

Thanking God His office wasn't very far.

"Take off your shirt" he smiled and said,

He studied my chest as I lay on the bed.

I asked what is this stuff that's welling up from me?

Like no other fluid I have ever bleed.

Its shiny and bright but doesn't at all hurt,

And even though it flows a lot it doesn't stain my shirt.

I feel very different, almost good in a way,

Is that the first sign of dying? Man I really want to stay!

He looked at me half smiling, half looking over his glasses,

As he touched the shiny matter pouring from me like molasses.

He said, "I've seen this before it seems as people begin to grow,

God releases something in them the name you should know.

"It's oil".

Oil?

"Soul oil" he said.

Soul oil?

"Oil from your soul instead".

Looking a little confused, dumbfounded and stranded,

He patted me with his hand, and said I would soon

understand it.

That the oil that poured deep from within me,

Was from the well of purpose God dug you see.

Although we all have one it's very rarely seen

Most die and miss the chance fully all to be.

You must have been praying

and really in your word,

For Him to really trust you

with these gifts I have heard.

A swell of relief washed over me quick,

I knew he was right, so I no longer felt sick.

Now that I look back on recent history,

There are a lot of things that He had given me.

Like the sudden sparks of vision and creativity,

Sometimes ideas race through my mind like

bumblebees.

I have vision for things to build

and to suddenly see done,

What others view as work is to me, simply fun.

I see plans in me, books in me, inventions

its' all true,

It is flowing so fast from my chest,

I don't know what to do.

There are needs I'll meet, and people I'll help, and I
will even show,

The direction that a fallen mankind

really needs to go.

I left his office after thanking him for the wisdom

he placed in my brain,

I knew that life as I knew it

would never be the same.

One day while in the shower,

Yes much less than an hour.

I heard a scream from the other room,

That shook the house like a sonic boom.

My son burst in wide eyed and said,

"Dad what's this mess"?

Pointing to the shiny substance

coming from his chest.

It's oil

"Oil?"

Soul oil, I said.

"Soul oil"?

Oil from your soul instead.

Angel

The Angel of our lives is beautiful.

She strikes our mind with splendor and grace and persuades us to go on when all seems lost and hopeless. We respond in kind with tears and smiles as our heart lightens. Her smile is reassuring and true. Her words have become her own, and we listen like children for as long as it takes. As long as it takes.....

Have you ever been hugged by an Angel?

Oh my!   Her touch is like the warm breeze and turquoise waters of the tropics, and if you close your eyes for a second you are there. You feel, as she holds you, the tides draw in and out from your body and the warmth of the son on your shoulders.

If I had to describe her embrace, it would be like the grabbing of my mind to jazz for the first time; or the peace I feel after a prayer; or the calm relaxed feeling during a summer's rain. It's the dawn songs of birds. It feels like the beauty of spring blossoms, or inhaling the intoxicating aroma of jasmine and roses, or even the sudden smile of a baby.

It feels like you're hugging heaven.

And we see her tears. She doesn't believe it. But we grieve when she grieves, and cries when she cries. We don't tell her enough but her love seeds connect us and continually produce love. We love her so this Angel, and we struggles when she cries....we hate it so.

It's not easy being an Angel. There are denied desires and 3:00 am meetings with God. Unrealized dreams and fights with the whisperings of negativity that tries to tell her who she is not; pillows soaked with the tears and crosses she and only she can carry. Sometimes she carries ours....

We do not know how she does it, but what would we do without her?

And so we pray;

"Dear God, please continue to watch over our Angel. Keep her mind and heart in your arms and hold her as she has held us. Make her to always know that even though we may not say, she is so valuable to us and you love her more than can be written. Make her to understand that the weights

137

are for making her stronger and a promise from you

is sure…in your own time. Her concerns are your

concerns, even the little things that she thinks are

insignificant and not prayer worthy. They are as

bigger in your heart than in hers. Bless her beyond

her comprehension. Keep her past temptation, and

fill her more than she thinks her heart can contain.

We thank you for her smile, her embrace; your

words and her petitions at 3 am on our behalf".

Amen!

THE WARMTH OF THE SON

(hummed melody) *slow, with feeling*

humm hmm hmmm,

huhumm hmmm huhuhm

I angle my face to the sky,

So tired of asking why.

Things haven't gone my way,

Even though I prayed.

Have patience I have been told.

Try and weather the cold.

It's been so long since I have won,

And my shoulders weigh a ton.

139

I need the warmth of the son.

(Hummed melody)

Not knowing where to go,

Where I feel I can flow.

A prisoner of time,

Who still doesn't really know his crime.

I eat, but yet I still,

In hunger, I still feel.

Being cold and tired is no fun,

Searching for life on the run.

I need the warmth of the son.

(Hummed melody)

There just has to be

A better life, just for me.

A plan to ease my troubled mind,

Some help to ease my burdened mind.

I've searched all over in vain,

But I cannot see through the rain.

Is there anyone listening beyond the sky

Who would be kind enough to hear my cry?

Being cold and tired is no fun,

I need the warmth of the son

(counter melody)

His love is warm…

Sometimes my visions not too clear.

His love is peace…

And often I don't hear.

His love is kind…

The lesson taught to me by pain,

His love is real…

Is really for God's a gain.

His love is patience…

Else I really wouldn't know.

His love is near…

It is not my sorrow to hold.

His love is love…

It never fails to last.

It is so complete…

The pain from my past.

It is not said for fun,

Or a fashionable ryhme or run.

I cannot make it on my own,

I need the warmth of the son.

The Healing

If I could with simple rhyme and verse,

eliminate all the pain and hurt.

Erase confusion with simple prose,

or pray words to God for all of those,

Who've used me, and abused me.

What if it's such a simple thing to teach,

to introduce the concept of peace.

Many have searched in vain to find,

that thing that would calm their mind.

Seems impossible!

Open we must reach beyond,

material things of which we are fond;

Unorganized thoughts and mental scatter,

to the heart of issues that matter.

Attainable?

Desirable?

144

Get down to the depth of who we are;

past our will, our sight, our emotions and scars.

To ugliness we dress up and hide;

with makeup, swagger, fake smiles, and false pride.

Lost little grown boys…hurting little grown girls

Tomorrow is just a day away

(A Song of Hope)

I guess it's true what they say,

about when you're going through.

It is so hard to see things in time.

Hard times seem to last forever.

But even if you are stretched to the limit,

know it won't last. Hold on to the end.

Don't give up or believe a lie,

although you can't see the sun.

Because as always,

Winter lasts for just a season.

Seasons always change.

Change moves us closer to our blessing,

And tomorrow is just a day away.

The days are hot, and the nights are so long,

when will it all just go away?

Is it my imagination?

Or have I been in this storm for so long?

One day I am up, encouraged,

then down; a victim of all my fears.

So alone, I feel the pain in my chest;

so very hard, so very cold

Then I remember,

Winter lasts just a season.

Seasons always change.

Change moves us closer to our blessing,

And tomorrow is just a day a way.

Bridge;

I can feel my deliverance come

with every ray of the future day sun.

Shining over the hills and every tall tree,

blessing me, restoring me better than I imagined.

I'm so glad I didn't give up.

I stood my ground, and cried but pressed on.

I am not ashamed to say that I wanted to give up,

and nearly forgot who I was.

The evening bed could have been my grave,

and self-pity my last meal,

But I held the hand of God,

and in his hands I was held,

So now I know with great surety,

Winter last a season,

Seasons always change.

Change moves us closer to our blessing,

And tomorrow is just a day a way.

Weeping may endure for a night,

But tomorrow is just a day away.

In the Beginning...

If I should Pass

If I should pass

Give my heart to the wind, to the back of a runner,

And let him cross the finish line.

Give my lungs to a storyteller, so no one will forget.

And my feet to justice.

If I should pass

Give my vision to my children,

The thousands of them;

My mind to invention,

My soul to God.

80

Man, I can't wait till' I am 80. I know it sounds strange, being so many years before the time; but I can't help but smile and silently chuckle at the thought.

When I become eighty, I will be the coolest old man on the planet. I will be a trim 225, stand erect, with broad semi-muscular shoulders. My stomach won't be flat, naw that's not me. I'll have a slight bulge but not ugly; and my face will be adorned with a snow-white goatee and eyebrows. I'll wear those smooth, thin, round frame sunglasses with a blue tint. You know, the kind you see in the movies. I'll wear a loose fitting, long sleeve dress shirt, with the sleeves rolled, and no tie of course; in subtle shades of blue and green. My double pleated pants will hang from my hips with a plain leather belt, and the crease will be so sharp I might cut myself taking them off the hanger. And oh yeah, I'll crown myself with a white panama hat, and comfortable but shaaarrp shoes, made by Stacy, or Geno… sumthinornother.

When I'm 80, I'll step out into the warm night air; look across my brownstone, jacket flung over my shoulder, and announce to the evening, by my presence I am coming. "Hello Mr. Man. How you doin' Mr. Man?", will be what I'll hear from the two generations of neighbors. I'll smile and salute them with a wave or by softly touching my brim. The smaller kids, I'll flip some change, and delight as they giggle away towards the ice cream truck.

When I'm eighty, I won't need some big status symbol to drive. I'll walk to the curve and get in a drop-top Caddie or Chevy, something from the 60's or 70's. I'll slide into my shiny leather seats, turn the key and feel the rhythm of the horses running free, as I grip the huge wheel and turn into the night. I'll listen to cats name Coltrane and Stitts do their thang, intricately weaving melody with form. Or maybe I'll listen to some gospel, if the spirit hits me. I'll ride down the street aware of everything. I'll lean back; one handed, as the cool breeze commands. The neon lights will be my map, as I turn into my favorite sidewalk café. I'll drink overpriced drinks called frappes and lattes, or my favorite fruit smoothies; and talk with cats name

Basil or Samuel about sports, or the state of the world.

When I get eighty, I'll use words like panache. I'll say, "you know that Joe", or "one thing about Joe, he's got panache". Or cosmopolitan, "you know Juanita she's quite cosmopolitan". I'll speak French or Latin. I'll teach a classroom without walls; read poetry out loud, and voice my opinion with a little more class.

When I'm 80 I'll sing a song I wrote to my wife, in our favorite dining hall or café'; then we'll dance and laugh and do what young lovers do. I'll answer her call with a smooth, "yea baby".

When I'm 80, I'll throw the biggest parties you've ever seen. I'll have a live jazz orchestra, and lavish meals prepared by French guys whose name I can't pronounce. I'll send for brothers who I haven't seen for a while and are a little down on their luck. We'll talk about old times and who didn't make it this year. We will eventually end up on the veranda overlooking the sleeping night and thinking aloud how good it is to be blessed, and how close we are to heaven.

To Hell with Death

Death has no imagination.

He wears the same clothes,

Day and night always,

and has forced many to dress up,

In rarely used Sunday Suits,

Or substitute club gear.

He's an anal fellow,

The bastard that he is.

Always on time,

Never late, but sometime early.

He drinks deep and long.

His thirst never calmed.

He's tortured the lost

With his threat of coming,

Causing many to tear,

And wished they had lived a better life.

I thought I pissed him off,

By slipping from his grasp.

But he was incapable of anger,

Or his plate was so full he didn't notice.

Before I Die

Every man I am to birth

has to hear my wisdom first

Before I die.

My footprints will not be filled with blood,

but of my story mixed with mud

Before I die.

There are a number of people I am to reach,

And so many to direct and teach

Before I die.

There's only one home I have to build,

But many foundations I am to instill

Before I die.

Some relationships to mend,

Reconciled with some old friend

Before I die.

Some languages I am to show,

New places I am to go

Before I die.

One last battle to fight,

Not fought with guns or with might

Before I die.

Maybe a leap to the sky,

In the twinkling of an eye

Before I die.

No more sleepless nights of why,

but peace so thick my high

Before I die.

A thing of Beauty yet to create,

not a forgery or fake

Before I die.

One last tilt of my head to the son,

His warm rays refresh me like the sun

Before I die.

A glorious ending of my purpose I wished,

Instead of dying… I am finished.

My Neighborhood

No Tears for Charlotte

Charlotte was a girl of modest looks at best. Painted to look better, trying to hide the scars deep in her face and implanted on her mind.

I see her with her aunt, or some foster parent, being cussed out at two years old and taught that the check they got wasn't worth the grief, wasn't worth the inconvenience of having to give a little love.

So they use her to buy their dresses or to go to the boat; or to put out their squares, or to empty out their lust on. They keep her alive so they could pay for their high, every third of the month. They don't kill her body, but they destroy the little girl in her. They starved her until she is always hungry, always searching, always looking for a way to feel good in her skin….

So who will cry for Charlotte? She's grown now but not mature. Don't mistake her smile for joy. She's still just a child. Her emotional growth stunted and stymied.

She walks on the street with no soul, having giving it away over and over and over. No one cares. They look down on her stained dress and bloody hands and say, "What a shame." But no one cries, no one judges to see, only sees to judge. She silently and desperately speaks, "save me" or "lie with me", not knowing the difference or at some point, not even caring.

I see her in school. Trying to understand how algebra was going to make her famous, and put her in a video next to expensive cars and exploitation stars. While she sees the curve of her back and the swell of her chest as her most valuable assets, thinking all she needs is the right outfit, or… all she needs is the right dance moves or… tricking the right dude to finance her right look. So she works on her back trying to make it; trying to matter, and hoping to feel good in her skin.

So who will cry for Charlotte? Not the church folks. They say, come on in but you must change first. You can't look like Charlotte the Harlot here. You can't show your scars here. Here you must act holy, because God only responds to you if you talk churchese. Elongated halleluiahs, and shatamohonda tongues, and falling out so they'll know you are for real. Getting up still dirty, and hearing a sermon, when what she really needed was a word, needed hope, needed to feel clean and good in her skin.

I see her dressed in white. Lying alone. Crying no more. No one heard her anyway. One or two people come to see her one last time. One person maybe, who tried to reach her; tried to get her to trust one more time; tried to get her to see that her healing and deliverance depended on it. Trying to convince her she mattered, and that God likes her and that God knows… and that God Himself was hurting when they destroyed her spirit… and that the way to freedom was to surrender to the very thing she trusted the least.

Someone painted her face to try to make her look better, to try to hide the scars deep on her face and implanted on her mind.

So who will cry for Charlotte? Or Charlie? Or Mike, Paul, Linda, Tamika, Joseph, Shaniyah, or Jennifer? Who will cry for Tatiana, Vicki, or Jamie? The kids, who through no actions of their own, exist. Who will speak purpose into their lives, pour into their lives, breath on them life? Who will tell them that they are beautiful? Not ~~because~~ a magazine with a limited and superficial sexual definition applied from the outside in, but because by the master's design true beauties' potential is unlimited, and flows from the inside out. Who will rescue them from the dark? The dark tongues and dark plans, the users and abusers. Who will help them see that pain is not a destroyer but a shaper? Who will teach them that one day they will grow and heal and help other Charlottes learn how to feel clean, clean and good in their skin?

Cool June

What a fool he is,

June that is

With his nonchalant stride,

not a care in the world.

Walking uneven,

captured by a loud beat only the simple can hear.

Drowning out common sense,

blinding him to wisdom.

Not in his eyes though.

The world is as he thinks it is;

temporary and short, indebted to him.

"Why is it late with my last check?"

He feels it owes him for being born.

After all, he didn't ask his dad to be invisible.

He didn't will his mom to be loose,

schooling him on how to be an evil man.

He was shown all his life

to look and act a certain way,

dress in style and talk in tongues other than English.

They're romancing him hard now.

They won't tell him it's over at 21.

He'll get a 'Dear John' letter

in the form of prison, death, or worse, mediocrity.

But right now June is dressed for June.

Living for June.

It's nice.

Perfect for fishing for little girls,

spawning little June Juniors,

paying forward the curse.

It will even get hot for a while,

perpetuating the myth that there is time.

When the last leaf falls off the tree,

he won't hardly notice.

By the time its freezing he'll be angry

…but won't change.

Naw, that boy will still be dressed like June.

Conversation

I talked to a young brother

whose faces was all in throthers

With the anger of man

With the anger of a man.

Misplaced aggression

with no purposeful confessions.

Just some pain, with no gain

from family rain, he had attained

By heritage unsang,

Raising his voice in the end

While trying to convince the wind.

"I am somebody"!

I defused him with reason

or rather truth and not treason.

I saw his contorted face

go from anger to spaced;

a look of wondermentlighttation,

an epiphany from words,

Something special he had never heard.

Nothing to it, nothing to it,

Once he thawed and thought through it;

Nothing to it nothing to it,

Once he thawed, there was nothing to it.

You see most of the young brotherhood

Gathered on corners of unpurposed fortitudes;

Rude and crude,

with dark deeds and troubled moods.

Mama didn't pop the tit out their mouth until 19 and

a half you see,

Dad sent a message from prison sayin'

"man please, just don't be like me"!

The anger rushed in to fill the emptiness,

the darkness or the absence of direction;

Leaving only erections,

or "I probably ain't gon live long" anyway

perspectives.

175

So they screw and howl at the moon, and when real

men try to calm them with love,

They see them as soft like doves;

Not seeing the purpose, not understanding the

strength of love.

Real men grab collars and embrace them,

put their hands over young brothers' mouths like

braces.

They stand making them sit to listen and to watch.

Sometimes they shake a young brother with words

that ring unfamiliar because they are truth.

Nothing to it, nothing to it

Once they thawed and thought through it.

176

Nothing to it nothing to it

Once they thawed there was nothing to it.

You see, boys sing songs of dying,

Smoking weed and prison mindset buying.

Keepin' hard blank faces to hide the fear,

The lost dream, the tears,

Shed at night when no one's lookin',

Only your girl know you been tookin...

On the ride of the lost,

with the cost of your future unsutured.

Causin' frustration and lamentations; dream
castrations, wasted playin'

play stations blank faced but you are angry and hear

the voice of your abyss,

trying hard not to give in but you pissed.

Yellin into the void "free me"

but its absorbed with no echo so you screw and

howl at the moon.

Letting loose lead until small bystanders are dead,

then you're overcome by the dread.

But is it all a dream or much the same as it

happened to your boy Hakeem?

No self identity, no remedy, no reflection kin to me;

No hope, no rope, lost and depressed, can't cope.

Talkin trash, giving the illusion that you know,

but what's hidden

Is an empty pot with a top

and when opened nothings been poured in it.

So the cauldron is filled with hate,

anger, and frustration,

The world closing in on you,

no dreams or imagination.

A freezing fire that won't die

that time demands will boil over.

Not a prophesy but a statistic,

the opposite of finding 4 leaf clovers.

Nothing to it nothing to it,

Once they thawed and thought through it.

Nothing to it nothing to it.

Once they thawed there was nothing to it.

So when you redeemed man,

encounter the nation of the lost,

Remember your past,

and how you didn't count the cost.

Time, age and God slowly revealed to you your true

life's purpose,

Not just for your gain but to sow seeds in young

versions of you and birth this;

Arising new population, this remnant, new young

vessels risen from the tomb,

Young men who want to be poured into because

nature abhors a vacuum.

Fill them with words of purpose, destiny, because

they are not bastards,

Focus their passion and energy in the direction

intended by the master.

Shine your light in and eventually their light will

.come on, and;

Dispel the anger, the darkness,the folly and

duplicate themselves like the sand.

Nothing to it, nothing to it,

Once they thawed and thought through it.

Nothing to it nothing to it,

Once they thawed there was nothing to it.

Remembering Dusable Street

April 19, 2006

Whatever happened to Dusable Street?

That great street

That marks the center of town.

The one nicked named state

To hide it's birth

Like a bastard child

as if conceived by sin.

But he survived them.

He sent for His kin in the south

and rested them in daddy's belt.

His black belt,

182

And they grew strong

And fought wars

And scared them with their resilience.

So they plucked up the harvest

And planted them North-west

and fed their children.

Far from brown hands that work

Hands searching for identity,

Unprotected they were.

They repaved your face with needles and rocks,

Causing paralysis and sleep.

Dreamless and low

It's all gone now.

Dusable Street is no more.

That great street

The one they nick named state,

They saw you as ugly but valuable.

So they tricked out your children,

And erased Roberts' homes;

And opened you to other children

The children from the northwest.

Parade of Babies

No music except the sounds of giggles from

children

As they pass by my window, dozens of them.

Fashionable are they dressed in ignorance.

What was their hurry?

They parade by thick and over mature

In body only.

Wearing mid-riffs, exposing proudly their folly

In the form of stretch marks.

I become confused.

Who is the child?

Who is the mother?

I cannot speak it

because of my sadness.

The shame they should feel

But they are comfortable.

Their grandmothers, not 38 themselves,

Their fathers' unknown, or playing basketball.

So young, so beret of wisdom,

Wisdom reserved for maturity.

Maturity they may never reach,

And so they march,

Ignorantly, proudly by my window,

186

Pushing a baby

While being a baby themselves.

The Hype

Thursday was usually a rough day for Chase. It was particularly brutal this Thursday. He felt its punishment throughout the overly crowded train ride, and the tense drawn out day of meaningless work for people he didn't care much for. He was a hard worker, said the right things, and seemed impressive beneath the watchful eyes of stiff white shirts and the latest power ties.

Chase stumbled awake this morning, assaulted by the patented low rhythmic shrill of his clock radio, and opened his eyes faster than they focused. The huge, red neon numbers sharpened and sneered at him for thinking it was later than he thought, and that he had escaped. He cussed in a low muffled tone as his eyelids lowered, then opened and repeated. His brain calculated hundreds of reasons as to why he should or should not go to work but settled on one. He had already missed too many days and was on the bubble. Clearing the crust from his eyes, he stumbled to his feet and into the shower, and was slapped by its hot spray. The mirror confirmed that he was still alive; a fact that he hesitantly accepted.

Chase reached the corner just as the low dull pain began to rise in the back of his head. He made his turn for the train, and detoured into the donut shop. The squat Indian man blankly took his order in an even monotone accented voice. His wife made the extra-large cup of black coffee, no cream, no sugar. She stacked it atop a napkin and placed it robotically on the counter. He didn't go in there unless he had no other choice because he didn't like the wife much. She seemed to look at him judgingly; as if jealous of the other days, days he didn't shop there and 'cheated' by buying coffee at the gas station. Chase grabbed his bag and chuckled to himself, amused that he had read so much into a simple look. He sipped too fast the steaming liquid, giving relief to his head but knowing it would not be enough.

The night had been long and sleep evaded him until about 4am. He hustled a few bucks, tapped out his debit card, realizing Wednesday night's high would have to last until payday. He embraced the lie and went away not caring that he would be stranded until payday, still two days from present. He was juiced and jittery, playing the streets until his high wore off; dragging him down as far as he was previously high. He did something that resembled walking, fumbled with his keys and made it into his place, to his bed where he slept in his clothes.

He would have made it through the day if it had been an easy day. The stress and his body's call for sleep made the clock's hand move cartoonishly slower than normal. Then there were his bosses. They slithered and crept around his workspace with evil eyes and malicious intent, making sure to be there when he made a mistake. He felt his nerves raw and screaming. He frequently visited the washroom, splashing water into his pale face. He felt a twinge of shame as he looked into his taunt sunken eyes. His mother had named him what she believed to be a wealthy person's name with the hopes that he would excel by osmosis. He didn't consider himself a junkie, but blamed his current situation on the pressure to succeed, which he never wanted, and on his mother. He felt his stomach tighten. The dry heaves would never come but the sickening sensation would seize his slight narrow frame. He began to perspire and shiver and his skin crawled with invisible bugs. His coworkers noticed. His pale white skin appeared damp and clammy. He told them he was probably coming down with the flu but a few knew the truth. He could not deny his urges any longer. The ache in his arms and gut could not be denied and he fumbled in his pockets for change. He could get a hit if not for being a buck fifty off. He rifled through his jacket, then every drawer of his desk until he was only fifty cents short. He lumbered to the snack machines, fingered the change as if counting for a cup of bad coffee and with perfect timing asked a coworker for the balance. After insincere thanks, Chase moved towards the ugly machine and faked patronage until the coast was clear.

He left work barely making it to five. He paced nervously by the elevator and pushed his way to the street where he turned into the rain. He walked six blocks. Past his train. Past the drug store. Past the church with the faded sign of "Jesus saves". He found his supplier and fumbled with the loose money as he handed it over to a kid who could have been his younger brother. The kid returned with the product, handed it to him with almost a look of disgust, even though he was a part of the chain.

"You gonna have it here man"? he judgingly asked.

"Yea, I'm uhm, just gonna chill over here man",
trying to sound younger than thirty something.

Chase sunk into the soft but worn chair oblivious to
the other users. He loosened his latest power tie and
stiff white shirt. Soon the stomach cramps would be
gone. Soon the creepy crawly feeling that parlayed
his concentration would dissipate. Soon the low
throbbing headache and sluggishness would fade,
replaced by energy. The energy of two suns. The
confidence of a king, or surgeon. He lifted his hot
earth tone colored cup and sipped on his double
espresso, worshipping the feeling as it washed over
his body and took him away.

U tink

Let me splain somtin' to you mon. somtin' your pa pa shoulda told you years 'go. You tink you da mon, dat you got a new game dat never been run befo'? I see you strut yourself down da block weareen da latest fashions dat someone don told you would make noticed. U tink lookin' the way you do, talkin' like u do make you an originale. I see U wit yo boys standin' around getting' old but dats all you can count is age. U tink yo schemes and fantasies gon come true by you runnin' yo mouth braggin bout what sumbody else do but not you? In fact U tink you the only one dat don try it yo way? U tink playin' just started? Dat popin collars don just got itself envented? Stoopid boy! Dey pop dey collars in the 40's wen dey put on zoot suits an danced on the ceiling at da savoy. Playin is timeless and simple, long as dare be silly girls. Speakin of which, young girls, u tink pretty just got here wit you. Dat maybe having big hips and a big booty make you special. Dat because da dogs chase you you special. Ha! As long as the little head do da tinkin men will always fall in love. But dare be millions of pretty gurls in da world. What you gon do ween yo beauty fade? How you gon keep him ween da babies round out yo curves?

Dare is hope though. Whoever liseen to da past will ween. Whoever take da heed of da good book got a betta chance. Dare nothing new unda da sun it say. Stop tinkin and start listenin. Don't be no fool forever. You have a purpose dat be bigga dan what you be doin' and a place in historee dat no one else can claim. Da man upsteers make your plan bigger dan sex, bigger dan hustling but if you don't respect him and respect yo self you wiil only follow da million befo you who only tink and not do.

Show 'em

I get it

Now I understand some of the purposes for the complexities in my life and I've made some decisions. Gone are the angry, frustrated twilight nights where my hands are soaked with the tears of hundreds of years of failure; what my daddy did, what his father did, and the weights of guilt and ignorance that held me away from my destiny, His destiny. Oh yes! There has been a nexus, a paradigm shift, a spiritual epiphany that has caused my eyes to dry and to moisten again, this time of gladness. To put it lightly...I get it.

I understand or rather accept the systematic placement and allowing of suffering and tribulation in my days; the strenuous breaking down of everything I know or thought I knew. Concepts and safety nets I built my pride on; a comprehensive complicated web of emotional and invested dependency in nouns; people, places and things; all crushed beneath the weight of truth in time and because I exited from blah, blah, blah and easy believeism and avoided the trap of nature and what it hates.

But I'm ready now

I whispered it at first, drew it back and then made it spiritual, a part of my soul. I heard a word, heard a word, heard a word! In my mind I heard a word. Bigger than the fool that is me: bigger than the wind and john carter and the mysteries surrounding my birth.

I stomped a negative thing to death and spoke it back with a word. Something in tongues: something unknown but to me and God. I kept speaking it until the fool that is me turned and said "It's possible". I allowed the voices of a Word to drown out my choir's old standards, 'What You Ain't/Can't Do?' and 'One day imma'. I worked and prayed and changed by A Word until my reflection looked more like A Word than me. I buckled then settled and refused to fear, not ever going back into the abyss.

I was free

I am becoming free.

The Run

One day I got the notion I could run. Having a lot of baggage and seemingly broken, made the task appear foolish, but I could not relinquish the thought. Over and over in my head I dreamed and visualized seeing myself different than I was; sleeker, faster, cutting the wind with my attitude, struggling and sweating, striking the ground with my feet, hitting it with my resolve, waging war against gravity, and all that I know to be common.

I started, slow and mechanical. First out of duty: the need to be right, to become the anti-blasé. Making my legs move forward, awkward, afraid of the trip, not sure if I was doing it right, only sure that it was right to be doing it. My body questioning the wisdom of my new mind, pushing past the fear, pumping my arms, finding the rhythm, the rhythm of purpose, the rhythm of time not gone by, but of what was not consumed.

And so I run. Past my flesh, past myself, past mediocrity, over the hills through long dark tunnels dank with the smell of decay. Through water, sloshing and slipping, stumbling but righting myself, using the hands at times to erect myself, correcting my stride. Moving not fast but steady, not hard but thorough, dependable, sure, like my father. Against the cold wind, rain of every color, soaking me, hurting me, building my character, and sharpening my mind. I reach out my arms. New, stronger arms; and began to grab necks, waking them up, dragging them along, erasing their ignorance until they find the rhythm of their race.

And so I run. Legs tiring, lungs hot and burning, breathing purifying fire. Throat dry, voice escaped, I began to think I was over. The scenery changed and sank below me. There was only the wind, lifting me, renewing my strength, giving me what I visualized, what I had heard about. I ran through clouds past where the sky ends, marveling at the carpet of lights. Only as a thought did I think to look down and back but I knew that I would see that thing that had been holding me back, telling me I couldn't run, that I was too fat or too old, or too dumb. I knew it would be slumped over, probably not on a hill but at the base of a mountain, having gone as far as it could. So I spread my arms and ran, eyes soaked with tears, glowing, smiling contently,

because in the distance, not far away, my heart sees

home, not far behind the narrow band of yellow.

Show Em

Something told me I wasn't going to make it

I squinted and dug in.

I called that thing a bastard

and dug in, ready for the grind.

I cursed it under my breath, and swore I'd show em.

Then I looked at my life.

I remembered the teachers, the family members,

and the wind

Who prophesied my demise.

Who prophesied my demise, and frowned.

They said "he doesn't have what it takes".

"He's not smart enough, he don't have the look,

he's too old".

It took me a long time to lose my hearing.

I narrowed my eyes,

twisted my mouth and bore my teeth.

I took a lesson from a cornered dog

and bore my teeth.

I bore my teeth, scratched the earth

and charged ahead,

"I'ma show em"

The Man and the Goldfish

Once there was a man quietly sitting on his deck thinking. He surveyed his surroundings, looking past the treated railings of his castle platform. Admiring first, then becoming in awe of the lush green carpet of trees and brush tailoring of the rolling hills of his countryside. He took special note of the all the variety of birds flying free, soaring high against the blue and white cloudy morning sky. They visited each tree, playing along with the symphony of wind and swirling leaves adding to its depth with high pitched songs. He sighed, as he inhaled the light aroma of roses, jasmine, and fruit blossoms that accented the streams of light spotlighting through the sparse fluffy clouds. He leaned back, hands across his midsection, and smiled peaceably, taking in his private paradise until his eyes fell close to a sun bleached table directly in front of him crowned with a large shiny bowl. In it swam a large big-eyed orange goldfish.

Stroking his chin and being a little melodramatic, he mused. How cruel the goldfish must have thought of him to bring him out of the house, and then tease him with all of this glorious view, only to deny him the pleasure of even swimming in the stream he probably could see below. Now he wasn't going to start the "free the goldfish campaign," shaking the vision of himself and three other losers picketing in front of the pet stores while wearing T- shirts that read, "Free Goldy" naw, that wasn't going to be him. Even still, he thought; why contain one of

God's creatures in this glass prison just for his own amusement.

After all, he was created to be in a stream or lake swimming free with his own kind. Instead, he was forced to swim in circles over dull plastic gravel and something that resembled a cave. He thought about this for almost an hour. After overly dramatizing in his mind the plight of this poor creature, he realized like the snap of the hypnotist fingers, that the fish had stopped swimming and hung motionless and silent in the middle of the clear water. In fact it appeared to be staring right back at him! Leaning forward in disbelief, he asked himself if he had suddenly gone crazy. He moved his body from side to side still hoping he was wrong. The eyes of the fish followed. He jumped to his feet and crept closer. The closer he got the closer the fish got in syncopation, until his nose was up against the bowl, and the eyes of the fish were as close. He fell back in shock across from the bowl and remained wide-eyed on the floor. Then just as he was beginning to adjust, the fish seemed to sign and shake his head from side to side showing his own disappointment in his owner.

Okay, now things were getting freaky. Beyond the initial shock he was feeling were new questions. "What does it all mean? What is he trying to communicate with me? God what does it all mean?" As if he was suddenly commissioned from on high, the fish's eyes widened and began to slowly look skyward. The man looked puzzled at first, but then began to understand. Just as he was looking at his surroundings, appreciating them, admiring what was done for him, he realized that he was content. God must have been looking down at him and feeling good about what he had provided for him. The security and love he had given. The joy the man felt. In fact he felt safe and free in his fishbowl. To let the fish go would mean he would fall prey to predators and have to search for food. The winters would be rough and he might not survive. As he pondered on these thoughts, he noticed his orange friend stare back for a second, seemingly smile, and then slowly swim away.

Love lost love

AFRIKA

I want to go to Africa

not to find who I am,

But to see where I've been

and bask in the beauty of blackness.

My soul cries for you Africa.

My heart misses your strength

being teased everyday by hope in the mirror,

while being betrayed in my consciousness.

I need the sustenance of your breast,

soft and full.

My stress falls away in your arms

and I become whole.

I need to go back to Africa.

I need the perspective of its sun

and the intelligence of its fathers.

My mind thirsts for its wisdom.

I feel I am a bastard without her.

The Question

How is it that a man is so strong and so weak?

Can fight an army but be humbled by a smile,

They sway of hips, and the whisper of soft eyes.

Can fall apart at the birth of his child,

and feel the room grow around him

as he shrinks at the awesomeness of it.

Is his strength an illusion?

A fabrication, a societal fable, he has to live up to?

Or is it more insidious than that?

Has it been written into his soul?

Imprinted across his spirit?

I would rather fight a war than think on such things.

I then could hide the fact that

I am only strong because I am so weak.

The Chance of love and risks

October 7, 2006

Broken hearts do heal.

Slowly and painfully they beat on,

With the help of God.

With the help of God,

Broken hearts do heal.

Once the memory is not an everyday domination,

And you smile more than cry.

You go on…and hope.

You smile…and hope.

More than you cry

Broken hearts do heal

You're blind when it breaks,

Sightless when it tears.

So you only see what you feel.

But every new day brings you closer.

Closer to being stronger than before,

And wiser!!!

But don't make the mistake of holding it

From the world.

And building a museum around it,

It's worth the pain to love again.

The Forever Man
November 22, 2011

It is completely reasonable to assume that you know that you are beautiful. It is, your beauty, the sum total of inward grace and delicate outward sweetness, sugar shaped and sang to like the sun and dew splashed on the petals of something red, purple or yellow. It's shaped and young and endless. It moves me, draws me in and sits on my tongue like fine chocolate and hard dark liquor.

But there is something else within you. It's a mist deep and hidden, beneath layers of history and red southern clay that feels like the bases of river trees carved with exotic languages. Out of the corner of my eye, between smiles and chocolate moods, it flickers and vanishes innocently. It is the spirit of the thing that I used to fear most; embraced now and hoisted like a cross. I come alongside you to carry it.

I will admit, I do not know you, this part of you so mysterious and pure. The part hidden in the shadows of your heart, but I will try. I listen as she slips sideways and shows her face beneath tiny fingers, painted with the truth of a word. I look away but listen. I look away but listen because I'm supposed to do what others have failed at. I respect the hope you have in God that I may be different, so I mash down my ego and hold open my hand. I bend and determine not to be the night that comes on cue as the sun fades, but be there for you all the time. I am the forever man.

So sing to me honey, show me your love. Unwrap it and let its covering silkily float to the ground. You don't have to be afraid. I will not recklessly laugh and drop your crystal heart. I will not place it on the table and forget to polish and warm it with my touch. I understand 'grace' because I do not deserve you. This epiphany fuels my resolve to love you past the true nature of the word. No matter how ugly your beauty, shaped so to throw me off from your deliverance. I will not run. So sing to me baby, while we dance close; feeling the rhythms in our chest mesh; holding each other so close; naked and in truth. Transfixed on each other's eyes; deep soulful looks into the heart of the matter; inhibition replaced with freedom, as your head drops and rests on my chest. We sway in the ambiance of your voice, up from behind your heart and far from eyes

and tongues and other unnecessary things.

The Dance
September 8, 2007

I tried to dance with my wife

But she prudishly asked what was wrong with me

and slapped me softly away.

Because she could not hear the Music.

I bopped and shuffled alone

holding her hand and waist.

Her frame motionless and disapproving,

Anchored by her memories.

But I didn't care.

Because I was free,

and my rhythm not circumstantial.

So I let her go and I danced in the same spot.

227

As she busied herself, I saw her sadness.

Not just because she couldn't hear the Music,

But because she didn't know if she any longer

wanted to try.

Funny Girl

August 5, 2010

Baby, I woke this morning with a smile.

Something you didn't say,

Rather the privilege of your presence…over coffee.

Feeling all teenager again,

thoughts of your smile

interrupting my morning tasks.

As my mind circled back to your hands on mine,

The closeness of our talk,

and your cute laughs at my silliness.

Honey, you got me singing love songs,

and thinking about your kisses.

But imma back off so I can see your beauty,

and know you;

unclouded by my feelings.

Sweetie, you make me grateful for moments

that pass so quickly, yet seem eternal.

Losing time in your embrace;

Mixing our hearts; making unknown beats;

and remembering the awkwardness

of a sudden kiss.

Girl, I respect your walk and who you are.

I won't destroy your smile with selfishness.

I wanna see you shine.

So make me squint at your brilliance

And dance in the music of your laughter.

Getting lost in your song, your giggles, and eyes…

Eyes that stop my speech.

What I heard was goodbye

"Okay, alright whatever you want is fine",

But there was no smile.

"You win, I'll do it your way",

But there was no heart.

Out the corner of my eye,

I see emotion has fled.

And what I think I really hear is

"Goodbye."

At home we move about in close quarters,

yet our hearts and minds are a million miles away.

Our arguments burned out just a little while ago,

and indifference really is its cruel stepchild.

But what I hear through painted smiles,

And false compliance for a while,

Is "goodbye."

231

When did things get really this bad?

It would be a shame

for my heart to lose it's

other half.

Maybe God alone can turn our hearts again,

An ember left, can perhaps begin ablaze.

We used to share our hopes and dreams,

But now, our fear is who we serve.

No more twinkle in your eyes,

Because I softly called your name,

And I think what I hear is

"Goodbye."

I'm afraid one day I will turn the key,

And the resolution of our actions will have come.

For her I want to be a better man,

For me I want her love.

God help us so we never say,

"Goodbye."

Echoes

Normally I would have heard the dim creak of cheap wood and rusty nails rub against each other. It was caused by the pressure of visitors, carefully climbing my stairs. It served in the past as a poor man's burglar alarm, alerting us to every welcomed and unwelcomed traveler ringing my bell. I was there, smothered by the numbers of people, and caught unaware, until the two-toned bell symphony calmly presented itself. I did not know who because there were so many already. I definitely did not know, or really care, where they would sit or even stand.

And so they came. On this day full of sunlight filtering through broad leaves of trees too old to do anything but give shade. The flowers bright and plastic. The sun hanging perfectly, and the wind as if on cue making its voice heard, pushing itself quickly through brush, trees, and vain daffodils, lining my driveway straight back to the garage.

Our house, my house, was old as houses go. It was racing, maybe limping to the century mark. Its foundation cracked, making it unsellable. Its porch long, wooden, in southern fashion, and plain except for the wind chimes casting their spells, of songs forgotten, and unappreciated. The house to the north lay larger and more modern in an 'L' shape. The house to the south, just as small and boxy as mine, but recessed back past my long driveway; even my garage. My house had by far the longest lot and backyard, going past the pink blossomed fruit tree of some kind and another 100 feet to a plain 8' stockade fence. Old houses offer no apology for not being fancy. Our front room morphed into the dining room, separated only by a one foot border. It was barely noticeable and just enough to qualify these sections as two. Past that, hung a wooden door darkly stained and crooked in its framing from many years of shifting and settling. It never quite closed completely. Behind it laid a better than average size kitchen and an old fashion pantry: a testament to days long gone, when mothers worked at home, cooking and caring. Beyond that, down steep curved dungeon like stairs, was a door to a dimly lit basement and the backyard. In the dining room to the right was an opening to the central hallway. Across from it was the bathroom and at its ends, my only two bedrooms. My family had done an excellent job of cleaning for me. It was immaculate, and better than we had ever maintained.

I was somewhat surprised at the number of people who filled our chairs, sofa, kitchen, bedrooms, and even backyard. Giving in to their real desire to relieve invisible tension with cool smoke, they puffed and talked in low muffled tones never rising above the crowd or through the rusting back screen door. Had I been in a different mindset this would have been interesting or maybe even humorous. I watched as I talked, noticing the reactions of the small cell-like groups. Talking to each other but seemingly watching me out of the corner of their eyes, hoping not to miss anything. They talked superficially of the funeral service, at least the older ones did. The younger ones did so but stopped when they felt me within earshot, as if it was somehow taboo. I could hear pieces of conversations like a few guys talking about basketball. I overheard flashes of talk about stuff purchased on sale, the weather, politics, more funeral service critiques and other small linguistic mosaics. It felt surreal and fake like the perfect sun or the plastic like flowers that lined my driveway. My words, though from my mind, my tongue and my lips felt unimportant and just for show. I struggled to smile politely, listening to their comfort, nodding my head as if grateful, more for them than for myself. I felt hypocritical but unsure why. I walked and was approached by person after person with words of wisdom and promises of reunions and assurances that this won't be the only time the family gathers. I saw my mother, strong and quietly whispering to her brother, my uncle, short of words. Our eyes meeting briefly, reveling uncomfortably and still ignorant as to why, I steered my politician handshaking toward the washroom. I did not have to use it. I mean to say, there was no urgent message from my brain signaling a time to relieve myself, but there was a sense of anxiety. There was an underlying emotion buried, unlabeled, and on unfamiliar ground. I managed to slip by some young person. He was a teenager and I don't know why, but I did not want to talk to him. I felt a minimal wave of relief as I closed the door behind me. I stood in the small but exclusive washroom looking at the mix of newly placed white tiles, teal walls and wallpaper. We had taken pride in the antique tub with its clawed gold feet. The sides were painted a deep burgundy or wine with the lip rolled over in metallic gold, matching the regal legs and claws. I stood on the plastic tile opposite the modest mirror, facing a man I really did not know. I searched to recognize and catalog who he was now, and what he was feeling. I scrunched my face, trying to evoke any semblance of emotion, a feeling, any position besides indifference. I began to realize through my haze, through the low throbbing in the top of my head, that besides the minuscule relief I felt while closing the door, it was the only emotion I had felt in some time. I reached in the cabinet, swinging the mirror by my face; catching a glimpse of the rest of the room in its face and three fingered the bottle of pain reliever. I closed the mirror hoping that man would be gone, replaced with someone who knew something, anything: anger, remorse, frustration, self-pity or hurt. I unhitched the child proof cap and downed two capsules. Chasing it with water from my palm, while tilting my head back, I closed my eyes and swallowed; feeling for a moment something behind my eyes. Scared, I watched wide eyed but disappointed, only to soon returned to feeling blank; like the sleepless baggy eyed man staring at me. I continued to stare but something wasn't right. I just couldn't place my finger on it. Something was out of synch. Feeling no better but no worse, I turned to reenter the play. As I walked out of the washroom my uncle and I exchanged a few words. I turned with my back to the dining room to answer the call of the young man who I avoided earlier with no plausible explanation as to why. He asked how I was doing in an intelligent and caring way. I then realized where I knew him from. He wasn't of high school age at all, but first year of college. We hadn't seen him for a while and I had forgotten how close he was to my immediate family. His eyes saddened just a little, but he had a pleasantness about him as he thanked us for helping him. I felt good for a second. Over my shoulder to my right I heard a soft familiar voice call my name. I turned, feeling a rush of excitement that filled my chest with warmth. I answered as I had a thousand times before. "Yea baby", and out the corner of my eyes, as I was turning, I saw her fade. The room blushed quiet and I felt isolated and open. I realized I'd heard myself answer to a wife who was forever dead. The room was fixed on me and I heard a gasp, as my mind and emotions crashed and broke through whatever damn held it from me. Pain washed over me all at once. It was if the dead part of me had been plugged in. I broke with a noise I cannot describe. I grabbed my face and cried. My knees betrayed me, and I fell helplessly to the floor. I cried long and hard in scary intervals, holding my face, but unable to hold the flood of salty tears and clear thin mucus. My audience stood by, none supportive, all unemotional and blank.

I woke with my face soaked in tears. Still crying quietly, I looked over to see my wife sleeping peacefully. Grateful and childlike, I watched her from behind as I lay; her shoulders rising and falling automatically, gracefully, without effort or fuss. I felt the heaviness lift, replaced with gratitude. Neither contemplating nor analyzing, just a little scared but content. I carefully placed my arms over her back, contouring my body to hers. I noticed things I'd forgotten and hadn't noticed in years: her thick dark hair, her high cheekbones, and the peaceful and motionless way she slumbered. Her simple and quiet, elegance kissed beauty seemingly in chorus with the pre day birds chirping lightly outside our window, as simple as the morning itself.

The Story of Her

Girl what's your story?

I see you a little different than everyone else.

I wonder about the thin lines around your eyes.

They are not from age.

They are part of your beauty.

They accent your eyes and tell a secret;

That there is more to you

They help the twinkle when you smile,

Or the blush when something's true.

Girl what's your story?

I know there's more to you than your curves,

Your perfect shadow,

that perfectly hangs your clothes.

What did you endure as a child?

How did you make it through all that?

I bet they didn't know you were that strong

Girl what's your story?

How do you cry and laugh at the same time?

How do you make 'simple' fashionable?

How do you hold secrets close to your breast?

…and trust in only what your heart tells.

Kindness so gentle, so rare, men take it for flirting.

Your flirting is so subtle,

it is artistic in its presentation.

What has your past taught you

that makes you so careful?

Was it your mother, or a careless foolish father?

What secrets will you take to eternity?

I see you think on them for a second,

between smiles, and I wonder.

How deep is the well and

how bitter and sweet is the water?

Something to Say

November 11, 2006

At the end of the day

There are so many words left on the table

Unspoken love and Infatuations

We fear what we cannot imagine

So we dream, and slap ourselves back to reality

And search in slumber for answers.

At the beginning of the day we're strong and sleepy,

driven by purpose and lust.

Gaining steam throughout the day,

Gathering more words

To leave embarrassed on the table.

249

Love Lost Love

A really old African told me this story:

Many years ago in a village with no name, in the shadow of Mt. Kenya, lived an old blind sculptor of wood, who appeared in the village only a few years prior, who no one really knew. His empty eyes sat above his squat, wide nose, and scraggly snow white beard that he scratched occasionally. His eyes protruded with large dark pupils. With knarred rough hands worn from years of gripping knives and forcing his vision against the bark and grain of hard, dry wood, he worked silently in the shadow of the great mountain, under the acacia tree, away from the villagers undisturbed.

Although he was blind, he possessed the amazing ability to sculpt from wood, beautiful, life size women that from a distance looked human. As legend has it, the detail was great and unimaginable. The hair seemed like wool and not wood. The texture of the skin was lifelike and you could almost see a story in their eyes. Hauntingly deep and mystical eyes that reflected the sadness or joy in the face of the women set in seamless linen and jewelry. People starred for hours and sometimes cried. He worked amidst the beautiful Acacias and baobab trees, using their wood to free the women from its womb into life. This went on for years with the occasional tourist stopped and stunned by the sheer beauty of his work. Many begged and offered great sums of money and treasure to purchase just one but he would never sell them. Occasionally he would give one away, the receiver or never knowing why they deserved such a gift.

One day, according to the African storyteller, he started another one. He worked without pause on this one. His hands moved slowly, caressing and shaving the massive piece of copse. He worked in both the sun and moonlight and no one saw him eat or drink, just occasionally rubbing his trembling old hands momentarily, then the slow "screep…..screep…..screep" again as wood submitted to the will of his age old blades. After awhile it began to take shape. No one was surprised that once again it was a woman. However, this time she was older, yet still stunningly beautiful. It became obvious that she was sitting or kneeling, but the old man forbade anyone to come closer or to inquire about its finish or identity.

Sometime later during the harvest moon the scraping and polishing stopped. As the sun climbed over the great mountains and pierced the veil of thick trees, the villagers slowly rose to find the artist finished with his greatest work of all. He had finished under the large Acacia tree a statue of a woman of unbelievable beauty. Her face and eyes were forgiving and some say angelic, as her loving and approving demeanor smiled down. She wore a flowing traditional Kenyan garb of purity, but this is not what brought the villagers and visitors to their knees. As they slowly inched closer and the shade from the tree fled the cresting light of the sun in the high horizon, you could see the sculptor lying

253

motionless against the breast of the woman he had sculpted. Her garb and breast was shaped and indented to reflect the pressure from his face, as if she was alive while his face was nestled against her and suddenly turned to wood.

His right cheek and head melded into her chest perfectly. His left hand lay motionless around her waist, as did his right arm the other way. Somehow…somehow, according to the villagers, her left arm was cradled across his back and her right hand rest just below his cheek as if to catch or wipe away the tears that streaked down his face. She knelt as he sat partially laying into her arms. No one moved. Many wept quietly, not out of sadness but from this miracle of beauty created out of love.

She held him tightly. While that morning, no one knew how to free him, or whether they should.

Over the years there has been much speculation as to why the old sculptor sculpted only women and how he came to end his work in such a fashion. Some say it was because he was just old and lonely, and fantasized about having a love in his life. Others thought he still mourned the death of a mother from which he had never recovered. Others thought he was just insane, and lived in a world that only made sense to him. However, most gave in to the thought that we may never truly know.

I have thought about this story often over the years, as I worked, or in my quiet times, but it wasn't until recently that I believe I began to understand it. You see, I believe the old man didn't sculpt many women as they thought, but rather only one. He saw in blindness what most men never see with their eyes. Those women, however simple they may seem, are very different and intricate. Their beauty is often reflected differently at various times, and they carry with them the range of emotions and feelings as vast as the colors of the sea. Maybe their constant changes in clothes and hairstyles reflect the inner, ever changing or churnings of strength, stamina and beauty they possess. Maybe the old sculptor once had a love that was deep and unexplainable. An inseparable friend whom the sun had set and rose on in his heart. Maybe they shared long days of working and talking, followed by nights of unbridled passion. Occasionally he would give one away, possibly to an inquisitive couple whose love he felt as they asked about his work. Maybe it reminded him of a love long lost. Maybe she was a love he allowed, for whatever reason to escape, without taking a chance, and the imagines were of his regrets set to life.

As for the moral to the story, maybe it's simply that love or true love only comes once in a lifetime. Maybe we shouldn't let our fear, or others opinions cause us to miss the one that will bring us a lifetime of companionship and joy. Even throughout the pain and suffering we experience, maybe it's just a matter of how we allow ourselves to see it. Or maybe...it's when you find that special woman, you should take her and through love, build her up and shape and polish her until your love reflects a great work of art for all to see.

I Was Not Prepared To Love

November 10, 2009

I was not prepared to love her.

I rushed into the room, blind and flush and said I do, made babies, slept and stooped, unprotected from my ignorance.

The years went by, and I learned slowly, meticulously, that love, or rather the fantasy of it, did not exist. It was a construct of the wind, as touchless as the wind, made erotic and physical and intense in my eyes, but I could not see her. She became invisible and would not show herself because I thought I already knew her. I'd defined love by her shape, lovely eyes, her complexion, but

258

she was not love. Time exposed my ignorance, and the truth destroyed it.

I was not prepared to love her

Nights of trying to figure it out or trigger some responses for my own ego, so I could believe we were one, but in truth we were three: I, her and the history of long dead men who hurt her, who did not love her, who hurt my grandchildren, who got high off her pain and made her carry a cross. They lined the streets of her mind and taunted her esteem as it walked by, spat on her self-image and caused her to stumble and sit in bitter pools. They caused her mouth to hang and her eyes to darken, making it impossible to enjoy life, to be satisfied with breathing, to like the rising and falling of her own breast. She would not trust again but I wore her down, made promises (unknown to me) to heal her, solve all her problems, provide sustenance, and to die for her but...I...wasn't.......prepared.

 My father refused to teach me so I rushed into the room, blind and flush and said I do, made babies, and slept, and stooped, unprotected from my ignorance. I fumbled in the dark and fell short. I mostly missed the mark by substituting erotica for sensitivity, and improperly handling her heart because I did not know I had it.

Somebody told me that God wanted me to die for her like His son so I built an altar. I burned what was convenient, but not the flesh. Ignorance stood by me watching the flames ascend to the sky. Smoke and flames billowed in front of the windows, carried smoothly, in swirls by the wind, up past the clouds for everyone to see but God.

And the years went by. I grew and she changed. Gave charge to anger, and resented my past ignorance with venom and malice. Vulture-in-laws lurked an enabled her bitterness, cosigning a contract of long standing hate. I tried to right the ship, armed with my new mature sensibilities, my wannaberight right now passion, moving to gottafixitrightaway plans. I matured and eventually I did it the right way. Enlisting Angels, waiting and praying, loving hard and hoping past hope only to an end game. The realization of which was failure. Not my failure, but our failure, a failure, the failure.

God hated it

I think that I ended right, but righteousness in failure is painful none-the-less. I was woke and righteous and understanding and tried to win her back but it was too late as I waved at her from the street as her angry tearless face shrank in the rear window as the vultures drove her away.

Broken hearts shattered and stepped on by the crowd who didn't care that it came from our/my chest. A dream denied. God takes pity and picks it up. I rest my head in his lap secretly, away from the wind, and my vision blurred with tears. He tells me to look forward anyway and the charge of breaking that curse is placed on the shoulders of my progeny.

Sons prepare to love her. Daughters, feel worthy to be loved and more.

I once chased a dream

November 21, 2006

I once chased a dream,

Or fantasized about it

Holding her close to my heart,

tasting her soft shiny lips,

Inhaling her exhaust.

I stared into her eyes into the soul of the matter,

And wished I knew if it was right.

If she was a part of my purpose,

Then I could move from fantasy to dreaming,

And I wouldn't be alone.

I once gave chase to hope,

Or thought deep and long on it.

Then stood to escape my fear

That answers do come in the morning,

And she wouldn't let me down.

Can I see her through my window?

Far in the distance, small an unassuming,

But beautiful.

Inviting!

Is her smile for me?

I once gave in to peace,

And stopped fighting.

I held her small frame in my arms and wept

On her smooth shoulders,

Washing her hair with old tears.

Feeling soft hands pat away anxieties

I stubbornly carried

For a hundred years.

It was just a moment really.

A healing for me to hope,

And the release of me to dream.

Something ADD

Produced

Spring

When spring shows up

She always makes a mess,

Wet, but still cold.

Making promises she rarely keeps early,

But she's still a lady.

Sending Easter lilies first,

Giving hope.

From our closets we welcome her with ceremonial

garbs,

Believing they will still fit,

Only to realize her great sense of humor,

269

As she laughs at winters jokes,

And not insisting he leave,

His welcome overstayed.

Even though we are glad to see her,

We rudely wish she would exit.

Our love for her is selfish and temporary,

Not appreciating her life's work,

Of waking buds, reminding the trees to bloom,

And painting the dull grass green.

Our hearts thaw to her whisperings,

Connecting us,

Arousing us

With Decembers dreams,

Made alive by her simple warm smile.

Free Away

Swing free away

Night breeze of city,

Too tired to run,

Too fearless to understand

Bondage in thoughts,

Tied hearts,

And damned.

Penance a gift,

Life ransomed,

Contracted vertically for the

First time.

272

Too strong to break,

Unimaginable the hold,

Fingers too secure,

Vision so strong, piercing minds.

Character converted,

Spirit set free,

Set free swinging

Free away.

Something ADD Produced

The only thing greater than my fear, is my ability to trust God.

If there is a shortness to life, it's because we only start to live when we wake later on the journey. Then it's actually full.

Life is only short if you never start living.

We matter not because of who our fathers are or because of our economic status and station in life, but because we are here. We have been allowed the victory of surviving. We cease to matter with the end of our existence if we fail to meet our spiritual imperatives; to except Christ as Lord and Savior, to live to help others, to die for a friend, to train our children for God's use and to maximize our experiences in this existence and die finished.

Most people try to be right instead of operating in truth. Never go for right, go for truth. In most arguments each party thinks its right from his or her perspective or view. They believe they are right. The argument is never resolved only ended. Truth is the only measurement for right.

Real friends are like gold. If you have a few, then you are truly rich.

Thank you for erasing my poverty

It's not that we do not dream as a people, it's that our dreams are stillborn or worse, some never even get pregnant.

Have we lost our humanity?

Three years ago, at Carver elementary school, located in the Altgeld Gardens housing community, I started a drumline. A few months later I began to hear from school staff and students that a new kid had transferred in that could really play. I auditioned him (after a week of him stalking me) and I was not disappointed. The kid could play. I learned later that not only was he talented but he lived, breathed and thought about nothing else but playing the drums. He graduated that year as a leader and our relationship continued as a social worker, mentor and even a mediator.

Tyler Ellis was not in a gang. He walked to the beat of a different drummer (no pun intended). He was not a straight A student and struggled to stay

focused on most tasks that did not require sticks and

rhythm. He attended the high school next door to

his former elementary school and walked his eight

year old sister home daily. I talked to him

occasionally after I ran a program at that school

every Wednesday with another group. He told me

he had started boxing at the park district and

carefully unfolded a schedule that detailed his next

bout. I tried to find time but couldn't.

Tyler wasn't the type to start a fight but was not one

to back down from one either. The last one he won.

It wasn't in a ring with rules so the kid who initiated

it sent someone back to finish it. A bullet entered

Tyler brain from behind. As he lay on the cold

concrete his killer stood over him and unloaded 5 plus shots into his body.

I visited Tyler in the hospital days later. I was confronted with my own helplessness as I stood next to his bed. Lights flicked and beeped, monitoring his vitals. Nurses and technicians worked in the background and I saw the strength of a mother.

We surrounded the bed and asked God for healing and restoration.

A week later or less I visited again. His mother had finally gone home. I'd bought a gift for his little sister. After a brief conversation with the nurse, I spoke to Tyler by his bedside. I told him it was going to be all right. I tried to speak as if he would suddenly wake and answer me. I prayed and ask God for favor. I told Tyler I loved him. I left and went home to my son. It was Thursday, December 25th: Christmas Day.

The following Monday, I texted his mom to see if her daughter liked the gift and to see how Tyler was doing. She texted back: "Well Mr. Smith, Tyler passed Friday at 9:33pm."

I've tired of living with the fear that I may know the victim of the next shooting. I'm tired of their funerals when I do know them. I am tired of the politicizing of a group's everyday reality. I am tired of the excuses, the lies and hearing why the solution is, depending on who's talking, somebody else's fault and responsibility. I no longer read the post of people on main stream news blogs. They don't get it. They don't try because they don't care. Racism is a sin that blinds and this country is consumed with the sins of ignorance, apathy and violence.

I thought hard about what to say at the funeral. I looked over the audience and my heart felt the pain of the dozens of teenagers there. Most were probably not affiliated with a gang in anyway but live with the sorrow of lost friends and family members and the reality that they may be next.

There were no cameras or media to cover Tyler's death. You see Tyler wasn't a model student and would not have graduated with any distinction unless his high school started a band program. We don't know what he would have done in the future, it was so unclear. He had not recently visited the White House like another well publicized young gun victim. I cried in the washroom at my job not because of his potential or his worth to the school, community or family, but because he was human.

Think for a minute; Tyler Ellis was a human being.

He lived and breathed thought and disagreed, laughed and walked his little sister home after school. Besides his family and friends, no one will cry at his passing. It became another news story flashed for a minute like the weather and traffic. It became an over exaggerated story in the neighborhood growing and changing after every telling.

But he was a human being.

God created us with characteristics that separate us from lower forms of life. We humans have the ability to think and solve problems. We are blessed

to infuse passion and morals into decisions we make

and are filled with purpose; not survival. Animals

do what they must to survive.

Humans have the ability to dream. To plan and see

goals develop into reality. We have the gift to

change, despite our start and to grow into

unbelievable people. We have the capacity to love.

Animals are affectionate and protective but that's

not love. Love is patient, its kind….

I cried because I'm human, because of the loss of

life. Tyler will no longer dream and plan. We don't

know what he would have become, what career he

would have chosen, who he would have married or

how God would have used him. He did not have the

chance to change and grow. That was taken from him.

And what about the gunman: most likely a child himself. What died in you so young as to execute another human being? To grip warm steel from your pocket, aim it and fire not just one shot to another human's head, but to stand over him and fire metal into his body until your weapon was empty. Did you sleep that night? I'm not asking because I don't understand crimes of passion, but I need to know that it's eating you up inside. I hope you are begging God to help you, to block out the images of that terrible act. I hope you are scared and crying. Not because of the fear of being caught or retribution, but because the weight of seeing life come to a standstill haunts you. I need to believe so because despite what has happened, you would still be human. Humans make mistakes, feel remorse and eventually repent. Even animals only kill when threatened to protect their young or for food.

I don't quite know enough about humans I guess. I don't understand how Tyler's death in a community is simply a whisper, fodder for gossip and then buried soon after him. Humans are compassionate, or supposed to be. I don't see much compassion towards a family when we have decided that the killer can walk around freely and the family has to move out of fear. How do you look your children in the face and not think that "this could happen to mine". Sometimes a 'snitch' is a brave person that cares enough to push past their fear so that they and others can live safe and free.

A human being

And while I'm venting, why are the schools in my
neighborhood receiving far less than others? Those
who are in power have read the same reports as I
have about the lack of a quality education being the
super highway to crime, unemployment and prison.
But in my neighborhood, the schools don't have
decent science labs or no science teacher, art or
design courses, architecture and business classes,
carpentry and automotive shops and music, choir
and bands. Tyler wanted a band. Maybe the gunman
would have been passionate about wood and
carpentry. So I wonder if you aldermen and mayors,
school board members and paid educators: have you
lost your humanity?

I wish that I can talk to Tyler again. I wish that I could assure his mother that although her pain is unmeasurable, she could be rest assured that his death sparked something. That it cause an epiphany in the hearts of the community and repentance in the minds of those who continue to create systems that nurture failure, death and imprisonment.

I will do whatever I can. I realized that as I spoke at the funeral, my college age son sat in the back of the church where I had been sitting. It was far from fair that just three and a half years prior, as he visited his high school for the last time to say goodbye before heading to college, that a gunman flashed warm steel hidden in his waste ban. It could have easily been my child's funeral.

It could easily be yours.

287